I0536748

BREATHE IN

By Michelle King

BREATHE IN

Copyright © 2017 by Michelle King.
All rights reserved.
First Print Edition: June 2017

Limitless Publishing, LLC
Kailua, HI 96734
www.limitlesspublishing.com

Formatting: Limitless Publishing

ISBN-13: 978-1-64034-795-3

No part of this book may be reproduced, scanned, or distributed in any printed or electronic form without permission. Please do not participate in or encourage piracy of copyrighted materials in violation of the author's rights. Thank you for respecting the hard work of this author.

This is a work of fiction. Names, characters, places, and incidents either are the product of the author's imagination or are used fictitiously, and any resemblance to locales, events, business establishments, or actual persons—living or dead—is entirely coincidental.

DEDICATION

This book is dedicated to all the women of the world who have survived abuse of any kind. You have faced a darkness and fear that most have not. Your heart and soul have overcome doubt, insecurity, and hopelessness. And in the midst of it all, you dug deep and found your inner warrior. You screamed at the top of your lungs to let loose of your rage. Then, when you felt your power again, you fought and remained true to your will to survive.

You are a force to be reckoned with.

*As the Phoenix eternally rises from the flames,
So shall she*

CHAPTER ONE

I grip the steering wheel and focus on my breath in an effort to steady my shaky hands. *Breathe in. Breathe out. I can do this.* I gaze up the long driveway toward the house through my car window. It sits tucked away from the road in a cove of evergreens. An immaculately decorative landscape sprawls before the stone home. Amber lights filter out of the windows, adding warmth to the otherwise cold exterior. It's impressive. Bold. Like Tom, it quietly exudes money and power. I've never been to his home before. He never invited me. Though it stung a bit, I figured he was waiting until our relationship progressed.

Even with a thin gray mist blanketing the scene, I feel oddly conspicuous. Am I the crazy stalker girlfriend? Have I overstepped my boundaries by looking up where he lived and showing up unannounced?

Groping through the contents of my purse, a sense of relief rises to the surface when I feel my phone. I hold my breath. *Please, please, please.*

1

As I press my thumb to the sensor, the phone recognizes my print and the screen comes alive. Scan notifications. One missed call. Click. *Shit, it was my mom.* Another kind of dread fills me. I'm not up for a conversation with her tonight. Click over to text messages. Two from Gerald. Scroll right past it. I'm not in the mood for him and his needy bullshit right now. Terin. I'll read it later. Scroll, scroll, scroll. Click back and forth, checking again.

Nothing from Tom. Disappointment swallows my entire being. My body grows heavy. Sour resentment rises in my throat.

Why is the wrong guy so relentless in his pursuit while the other blows me off? It's completely backward. How am I so thoroughly messing this up? Tom hasn't called or texted back in almost a week. He's clearly avoiding me. Maybe I had been too clingy before. Maybe I'd—

Stop. Just stop. Those are negative thought patterns. There's probably a good reason I haven't heard from him. He could be very busy with work. He could be out of town. Maybe he's not feeling well. That thought worries me. Maybe he needs help, someone to care for him?

My heart races, my movements are quick and jerky as I slide out of the Subaru Outback, pretending I'm not anxious to see him as I face his home. Why do I do that? Try to fool myself? I mean, how can one even accomplish such a task? You can't really, because it's...well, it's impossible. You're the one thinking the thoughts, so you cannot hide them from yourself. Yet, I try. Why

2

is this?

The banter in my brain is ridiculous. Two dichotomous personalities consistently bickering. Both of them annoying. Always. *Stop. Just stop.*

I shut the driver's side door and take in a deep, cleansing breath, closing my eyes and letting the day go with my exhale. I've been practicing this a lot lately. Breathing. Letting go. Sounds easy, but it's actually quite difficult for me. Every night for the last few weeks, my nightly ritual before bed has been listening to fifteen-minute guided meditations. I put my earbuds in, close my eyes, and listen to the gentleman's calm, hypnotic voice, telling me that regret is living in the past, anxiety is living in the future. Hyper-focusing on either is a waste of time and harmful. It causes stress, which can poison the mind and body.

Yeah, tell me about it.

So I breathe in and I breathe out. Letting it go. Except it doesn't work. A mixture of panic and anticipation breaks through as I walk toward his home, my heels clicking on the sidewalk. I stare at the French doors for what feels like an eternity before I finally knock on the door.

Moments later, the door swings open and Tom's confident presence fills the entryway. I both love and fear this about him.

"Tessa, what are you doing here?" He steps out of the front door and closes it behind him, as if he doesn't want anyone who may be inside to hear us. I shuffle backward and bring my arms in tight to my side to make room on the porch, feeling it necessary to make myself smaller than I already feel.

His reaction is a mix of surprise and disappointment and, maybe, a little anger? I'm suddenly acutely aware that I've made a huge mistake. I cringe and wish I'd never been such a stupid girl. "Tom! Hi." I clear my voice, hoping to bring it down an octave so I don't sound like a school girl. "I…uh…well, you hadn't answered my texts and I was beginning to worry. I thought maybe you were sick…or…I don't know. I shouldn't have dropped by like this."

"No. You shouldn't have."

His sharp tone has me taking a clumsy step backward. "I'm sorry. I…" Unable to finish my sentence, I wait for him to jump in and explain what is going on.

"How did you find out where I live?"

An uncomfortable silence lingers between us as I strain to find the right words, any words, to answer the question.

He shakes his head. "Never mind. This is my fault. I should have responded to your texts and just told you I can't see you anymore."

My head spins. The world tilts. A daunting thought washes over me. "Oh, my god, you're married." I want to die.

"Look, Tessa." He takes a step toward me, his six-foot-two frame reminding me how meager my own is at five-four. "I'm not married. I'm just a very private person. I always have been and I want to keep it that way."

"So that's it? You're ending what we have, just like that?" The pitch of my voice is embarrassingly high, but I can't seem to control the way I'm

4

escalating.

"What we have? Tessa, we've only been seeing each other for a couple of weeks." Tom stares down at me, his brows pinched in mixed emotions. I can't tell if he's sad, frustrated, amused, or just feels sorry for me.

A wave of embarrassment floods over me. My heartbeat pulses throughout my body, echoing the impending sense of doom that quickens my breath. "Yeah, but it was a great couple of weeks. Almost two months, actually. And we've been together almost every day since we met. I thought things were going really well. This is just a shock. I don't understand what's going on. If you're not married, then what? Did I do something wrong?"

He closes his eyes and sighs before answering. "It's not that you did anything wrong. It's just that I don't really see it going anywhere. Besides, what about that Gerald guy you were seeing before?"

"Gerald? I told you. I stopped seeing him after that first day you and I spent time together. He…he's contacted me but, I'm…Gerald isn't what I want."

"Look, don't make this harder than it needs to be. I like you. You're…sweet. But I don't have time for a fling. And you can't be here, so just leave."

I flinch at the bark of his tone. *I'm sweet? A fling? Just leave?*

Grasping for dignity, I take three shaky steps backward. My ankle rolls but I stumble and catch myself before I fall on my ass. Searing pain shoots hot through the tendons of my lower leg. My lips pinch to hold in the gasp of pain. Without saying

5

another word, I turn and bolt down the driveway. The slap of my shoes against the pavement reverberates into the cool air, echoing my shame. My ankle throbs with each motion. Confused and frightened, I slide into my car, start the engine, and pull away from the curb. My hands shake so hard I can hardly grasp the steering wheel.

What in the hell just happened?

Breathe in. Breathe out. Let it go. Tears roll down my cheeks in a steady stream as I drive away.

***

Parking across the street from my brownstone, I scan the dark streets before turning off my vehicle. Tom made fun of my fear of the dark. "You're too skittish," he said, "like a beaten dog, and you need to find your backbone. No one likes a wimp." Tom can be a bit harsh like that. Or as he'd say, "direct and to the point." Well, he was certainly to the point today. No holds barred. Doesn't change the fact that he's right. I do need to stand up for myself. I wish I had stood up for myself in front of his home earlier. Told him he couldn't treat me so terribly, at the very least. Like that would have done any good.

It also doesn't change the fact that these streets are a bit frightening, even during the day. I'd have never chosen to live in this part of town of my own accord. But when my grandmother passed and left the small unit to me, I had no other choice. As a student, still struggling to finish my doctorate of philosophy, I felt only gratitude for the sudden change in my living situation.

I'd just finished my master's in English literature and resigned myself to the idea that I'd have to wait to move on to the doctorate program when I received the news that I'd inherited the home. I'd no idea I was even in the will. Free accommodations are a godsend to a stressed and struggling student.

Grabbing my keys and purse, I wait until the street is clear of traffic. I note the glisten of the wet pavement from the earlier rainfall and my shoes don't have the best traction. I want to slide out of the car, cross the street, and retreat to the sanctuary of my home as quickly as possible, without slipping and breaking an ankle.

Ready, go. Open the car door. Step out, look right and left. Close door. Scurry across the street, making sure to keep my feet low to the ground for solid placement amongst the fallen golden leaves smushed against the pavement. Quick leap to the curb. Almost there. My keys slip from my fingers as my feet hit the sidewalk. Shit. I stop to pick them up. Out of the corner of my eye, movement catches my attention. My heart rate flutters nervously under my thin skin. Stooped over, I turn to see a woman standing at the curb about fifteen feet away. Nothing to worry about. My heart slows down.

I've seen her before. Thigh-high boots. No stockings or jacket, though it's cold out. Hair cropped short, in purposeful disarray. Clearly a hooker, she's decided this part of town is more profitable as of the last month or so, and frequents this area often. As I stand up and put my keys into my peacoat pocket, she turns and locks eyes with mine. She squints ever so slightly, measuring me

7

up. I wonder if she thinks I'm judging her. Am I? What must her life be like? What events have pushed her to a life of prostitution? How does she swallow the fear? Are we really so different, she and I? After the way I just let Tom humiliate me, like so many of my other boyfriends have, I'm not sure I like the obvious answer to that question.

Her lips purse together tightly as she shakes her head and turns away, as if disgusted.

I take in a short gasp. I'm the one who has been judged. She recognized my fear and it sickened her. Heat rises to my face and I hike my purse onto my shoulder before scurrying up the stairs, anxious to hide from this hideous day. Could it get any worse?

"Tessa."

Two stairs up, I stop mid-step and glance upward toward the male voice. My heart sinks. Things just got worse. "Gerald." My voice cracks. "What are you doing here?"

Gerald stands on the top stoop, staring down at me with a pathetic look of desperate hope dripping from his gaunt features. What did I ever see in him? Was I really that lonely?

He steps forward and offers me a hand. "Come on out of the cold and we'll talk." His voice has always struck me as oddly deep compared to his looks. Like James Earl Jones bred with Popeye's girlfriend, Olive Oyl, and Gerald was the result. I ignore his offer for assistance and remain rooted on the spot, staring up at him incredulously.

"Gerald, it's been a long day. I'm not up for company right now. I just want to go home and crawl into bed."

His lips press together so tight that they blanch white and the upper right side twitches. He gives an almost unperceivable nod of the head, as if clearing his thoughts, brushing away the rush of agitation. The previous look of calm concern returns as he offers a forced smile. The wave of anger that flashed over his features was so quick I almost didn't catch it. Almost.

He takes a step back and clasps his hands together, as if showing he's retreating and harmless. "I'm sorry you had a long day. Maybe I shouldn't have stopped by unannounced, but I began to worry when you didn't respond to my texts. It's been nearly a week since we spoke last."

I finally trod up the last few steps. "Gerald, I told you, I just don't see a future between us. I'm not really interested in a relationship right now." It's hard not to grimace as my words essentially echo what Tom just said to me only moments ago.

"You mean you're not interested in a relationship with me. But I know you've been hanging out with that new Tom fellow, the suit. I bet you want a relationship with him. Is that where you were just now?"

"First of all, I'm not in a relationship with anyone. And second of all, it's none of your business."

He blinks three times, as if suppressing another fleeting emotion. "So you're not seeing him?"

Closing my eyes, I rub my right temple and wish to God this day was over. "No, Gerald. I'm not seeing him. I'm not seeing you. I'm not seeing anyone." I look up. "I just want to go to bed. I don't feel good."

His expression softens. "You poor thing. I'm sorry I came over like this. I didn't mean to upset you. I was just concerned. Is there anything you need? Anything I can get you?"

"No, not really." A small part of me softens to his kindness. I wish I could muster feelings for this guy. He really is sweet to me when he's not being so overly persistent, so clingy. I just can't force what isn't there.

He hesitates. Looks down the street as if searching for what to say two buildings down. Looks back. "All right, well, I'd better be going then. If there's anything you need, just call."

I nod. "Okay." I just want to be left alone.

He traipses down the steps, pauses on the stair below me, turns, and places a wet kiss on my cheek. "I'll text you tomorrow."

I suppress a shiver. Please don't. "Fine."

I hold my breath while I watch him get into his car and drive away. Anxiety and relief flood my system as I turn and bolt up the stairs. The building is locked for the evening, so I scramble for the keys in my pocket and quickly open the door.

I love that wonderful, safe sound of the click as it locks into place. Push thoughts aside. Turn and walk down the hall to my door. Unlock and step inside. Yet another layer of safety as I lock both the handle and the bolt. I'm home.

In the sanctuary of my building, socks keep my feet warm as I pace around the kitchen, trying to make sense of today's unexpected turn of events. My cell phone sits on the counter silently, next to a plate of untouched cheese and crackers. I keep it close, just in case Tom calls to apologize or at least explain. He will, won't he? A siren screams in the distance and I pretend it's not there. Someone hasn't committed a crime or suffered a terrible injury. Too gruesome of an idea for the evening. I'm tired and a bit frazzled, but trying my best to find a calm end to the day.

A text comes in and I scramble to retrieve my phone from the counter top, knocking over an empty glass in my haste. *Mother* blinks on the screen. I close my eyes tight against ugly emotions: angst toward my mother's relentless nagging about my cheating father, and shame because I had hoped it was Tom. What is wrong with me? Sometimes I wonder if my consistently poor choice of men is due to watching my mom and dad's toxic relationship all through my childhood. The ups and downs, the ebb and flow of when things were good and then suddenly bad again, the constant feeling of walking on eggshells, of pretending it was all okay even though it never was. It certainly couldn't have helped.

My appetite has waned, so I clean the kitchen and retreat to my bedroom for the night. Peeling out of my slacks and blouse, I slip into a t-shirt and forgo the shower. I don't have the energy for it. The sheets are cool against my thighs as I slip under the covers.

Before I put my phone on the nightstand, I do the one thing that I know I shouldn't, but keeps nagging at my conscience. I pull up Tom's number and send a quick text.

Me: I just want to say I'm sorry. I shouldn't have dropped by like that. Good night.

Refusing to allow guilt or regret to slink into my thoughts, I toss the phone aside and sink down into my soft pillow. I remember the last time Tom and I spent the night together.

Lying in the dark with only the light from the hotel bathroom filtering in. The cool night air drifting in under the wispy curtain of our hotel room. Tom always insisted that a window be open. If a hotel didn't have windows that opened, he wouldn't stay there. It always struck me as odd. Only half awake, I ran my index finger over the tattoo that adorned his left bicep. "What is this?"

Sleepily, he glanced down. "It's a phoenix. Don't you know what that is?"

"It represents death and rebirth. Burning to ashes and then rising again into a new life. Right?"

He closed his eyes, drifting to sleep in a post-sex reverie. "Something like that."

I continued to run my fingers over the tattoo and imagined myself burning from the inside out into a heap of wasted ash and then suddenly bursting to life again into a stronger, more beautiful self. A self that speaks my mind and lives a braver existence. "I wish I had a tattoo like that," I whispered into the dark, more to myself than to Tom.

To my surprise, he answered without opening his eyes. "You have to earn it first."

Tilting my chin up, I watched his strong jawline against the pillow. "How did you earn yours?"

12

A pause lingered in the air between us.

"I don't like to talk about it, but my dad died when I was only three. After that, my mom went through a slew of men. I guess she couldn't handle the idea of being alone. Some were cool. Some weren't. One was a sick bastard that had a thing for young boys."

Another pause filled the air as I processed what he'd just shared with me. I gasped and my stomach rolled as I realized the underlying meaning of what he said. I placed a hand on his chest. "Tom, I'm sorry that happened to you. Did you ever tell your mother? How did you cope?"

His body stiffened in the bed next to me. His breathing was shallow and slow. "My mom knew. For four years, she knew and did nothing. As for how I coped, when I was old enough, I made sure to be there as a witness to their karma."

"What do you mean?"

He looked down at me, but his eyes had glossed over, his brow furrowed as if seeing something from his past rather than my face. He shook it off. "Nothing. I don't want to talk about it anymore." He rolled away, turning his back to me. His voice was gruff. "I earned the tattoo. That's all you need to know. Now go to sleep. I'm tired."

Now his words echo in my mind as I lie here in bed, feeling like a broken fool, wishing he'd respond to my text. This is my pathetic pattern. There is no possible way I could ever earn a symbol like that. I cannot be someone that I'm not, no matter how hard I wish it.

Shoving aside old conversations and images of a burning phoenix, I roll to my side. Click. The light goes out. Ear buds in. A calm, soothing, masculine voice tells me to breathe in and breathe out.

I am calm. I am calm. I am calm.

***

An obnoxious sound taunts me out of dreamland. I'm conscious enough to know I'm rising out of the depths of REM sleep, but out of it enough to resist. Limbs are heavy. Lids won't lift. Mouth is hanging open and dry. The sound is incessant, so I drag myself to the surface. Eyes open and close. Open and close. Open. Brain processes sound. My cellphone ringer.

Rolling over to the other side of the bed, I reach for my phone, hoping it's Tom. What time is it? A quick glance at the red digits of my alarm clock tells me it's only five after ten. I haven't been asleep all that long. Still, it's kind of late for phone calls. At least for me it is. Eyes focus. It's Terin. Oh, yeah, I forgot to read her text earlier.

"Hey, Terin, what's up?"

"Girl, you sound tired. Were you sleeping already?"

I lie back on the pillow and close my eyes again. "No. I mean, yes, I guess I fell asleep. But I'm awake now. What's up? I saw the text from you earlier and meant to read it, but I didn't get to it. Then I fell asleep and…it was just a long day, that's all. I'm sorry."

"Whatever, it's cool. You're super busy these

14

days. I get it. I was just texting to see if you were still pining over that Tom asshole, waiting for him to text you back."

This girl. She's the one person I can be myself with. The one person who has my best interest at heart. She's brutally honest, and sometimes that sucks, but it's always something I need to hear anyway, so I take my lumps as she serves them. "I'm not pining over him. Not really. I had hoped to maybe...I don't know, see him again. Have some closure?"

"Closure? I'm sorry, is him ignoring your texts and phone calls for over a week not enough closure for you?"

I cringe. There's no way in hell I'm going to tell her about tonight's incident. "Jeez, Terin, go easy on me. It's not that simple. I think I just got caught up in our little...*fling*." The words taste bitter on my tongue. "He and I had a good time and I got ahead of myself. No big surprise. I've done it before."

"So I take it you still haven't heard from him then?"

I sigh, contemplating how much to disclose. "Look, he's much older than me and I think that's always bothered him. Plus he's a very wealthy and successful businessman. He travels a lot and work takes almost all of his time. He said he likes his privacy and wants to keep it that way..."

"So you *have* heard from him?"

Her critical discernment is the thing I both love and hate about her. It births doubt within me. It reveals my stupidity. I pause and think carefully before I answer the question. "Yes. Today. He said

15

that he couldn't see me anymore. That he was a private person and too busy for…complications. That vague explanation is all he gave. I'm confused and a little heartbroken, to be honest."

She sighed loudly. "Shit, I'm sorry, Tess. I know I'm busting your balls here, but I love you and hate seeing you hurt. And if you ask me, he's hiding something. I have a hard time believing he was all hot and heavy after you these last few weeks and then he suddenly drops you like a hotcake and gives you a lame excuse about being too busy or too private, or whatever. It just doesn't set right with me. You know?"

I shrug. "I guess."

"Come on, think about it. His behavior has been off from the very start. I suspect he's got something to hide, but I never wanted to mention it before and kill your hopeful joy. It's been a while since I saw you that lighthearted and happy. I couldn't bear to rain on your parade. Maybe I'm wrong and he's just an asshole."

"I know you don't like to upset me. Plus, I wouldn't have listened anyway. You know how I am."

She gave a light chuckle. "Yeah, I know. You ostrich everything. Something crops up that you don't like and you stick your head in the sand to avoid conflict. Seen it a hundred bazillion times." She pauses a heartbeat. "Listen, I just worry about you. You know? I mean, you've always been so…"

I close my eyes, bracing for what she's about to say. "So what? Such a pushover?"

"Well, that's not what I was going to say, but

16

now that you mention it, yeah." Her speech picks up as she tries to recover. "I don't mean that as an insult, Tess. You know that. I love you. You're my best friend. But as your best friend, there are times when I just want to scream and pull my hair out when I watch you be so dang nice all the time. I mean, don't you ever feel like not being nice? Don't you ever feel like telling someone to shove it where the sun don't shine?"

I shrug into the dark room. "Not really. I don't think so. I don't want to be mean to anyone or hurt someone's feelings."

"But see, that's exactly what I'm talking about. Sometimes in life, you have to step on other people's toes just so they stop stepping all over yours. It's not always fun, although, it can be. But it is often absolutely necessary. You hear what I'm saying? Sometimes it's not an option. You gotta stand up for yourself simply because it needs to be done. Does that make sense? You feel me?"

I nod. "I understand what you're saying. I do. I just can't fathom finding that kind of bravado anywhere inside of me. Have I thought of speaking my mind? Yeah, sure. Can I act on it? Heck no! I'm not like you. I wish I was but, then again, let's face it. If I acted anything like you, I would have probably already bitch-slapped my uptight boss and been fired long ago."

The offhand comment has the exact effect I had intended. Terin sputters and spurts as she laughs into the phone. "Isn't that the truth? Oh, what I wouldn't give to watch you do something like that. I know it's in you, girl. Way down deep. You just

17

don't know it yet. And don't worry about that bitter woman, Tess. She just needs to get laid. Is she still giving you a hard time?"

"Nothing more than usual. She's a bitter, angry old woman and I'm the one she likes to take it out on. Story of my life. Reminds me of high school and the way Cindy Lorde used to make my life a living hell."

"Oh, jeez, Tessa, when are you gonna get over all that? It was a long time ago. And she's probably a washed up has-been by now with twenty kids and a big butt."

I roll my eyes. "Yeah, well, she was *the cool girl* back then and that's a perfect example of a time when I should have stood up for myself."

"That's true and further proves my point. It's time you started sticking up for yourself. So, back to the Tom thing…you're over him then? You're doing okay?"

I bite my lip and stare at the ceiling fan overhead. Mostly shadows in the dark room, its blades are still and my clock light reflects off it oddly in the center so that it almost appears to have eyes. It looks like a starfish clinging to my roof.

Should I lie or tell her that I'm miserable and praying he'll call me? I don't even know why. Like she said, he'd told me he *couldn't* see me anymore. Not that he didn't want to see me. Just that he couldn't. That thought makes me sick to my stomach. How could I want a man who no longer wants me? I bet Gerald would be more than happy if I called him tonight. Ugh, I'm such a stupid girl sometimes.

18

"Yeah, yeah, Terin, don't worry about me. I'll be fine. I, uh…"

My phone buzzes as a text comes in. Without thinking, I pull the phone from my ear to take a peek. It's Tom. My heart thuds against my ribcage. Hit the text. Read it silently, holding my breath while my friend rambles on.

Tom: Stop. Texting. Me.

That's it. That's all he has to say to me. Tears well up and I feel like I might choke on them. Swallow down the shame. Terin was right about him. I never meant anything to him. I'm probably one of many. Insignificant. I place the phone to my ear and listen to the last bit of whatever Terin prattles on about. I can't focus. When she pauses, I take the chance to escape. "Hey, I hate to cut it short, but my stomach is killing me. I think I might have eaten something bad. Do you mind if we hang up for the night?"

"No, no, sure. Sorry you're not feeling so good. Hope you're not on the toilet all night long. Remember that time I ate the bad clam chowder and nearly died from projectile diarrhea?"

No answer.

"Okay, I'll let you go then, Tess. Just call me in the morning to let me know you're alive."

Hoping I still sound cheerful, I say goodnight, hang up, and toss the phone to the foot of the bed.

I'm not even going to try to breathe through this. I stare up at the ceiling and let the tears run down my cheeks, into my hair, and onto my pillow. The starfish on the ceiling stares back at the sad, pathetic girl and laughs.

CHAPTER TWO

My right front pocket buzzes. A text message. I shelve another book and ignore it. It's probably Terin again. She's been serial-texting me for the last four days. If I respond, she'll interrogate me until I confess why I'm avoiding her. It's not like I want to admit that I'm depressed and in a funk because of Tom. It's not like I want to admit how pathetic I am over this.

"Tessa, when you're done there, would you mind helping this young man log onto our computers?"

Distracted, I give my coworker, Sara, a quick nod. "Yeah, I'll be right over." I adjust my blouse, pulling it down over the waist of my trousers. The boy looks to be about twelve and has his shoulders hunched and his baseball cap pulled low over his eyes. I flash a welcoming smile and wave him over. "Come on. Let's go. It's easy. I'll show you."

As I get him settled into one of our computer stations and demonstrate how he can log in and access the intranet and the internet, my phone buzzes repeatedly. The boy seems comfortable with technology and the web once he's logged in, so I leave him to navigate on his own. My pocket is buzzing every few minutes at this point, and I'm desperate to take a minute to give Terin a quick response so maybe she'll leave me alone.

I scan the floor. Gretta is nowhere to be seen and I'd rather not deal with her at the moment anyway. Sara is at the library's front desk helping check out a short line of customers. I stride toward her and let her know I'm taking a ten-minute break before I shuffle out the front door. The minute I step outside, I regret not grabbing my coat. Everett, Washington is experiencing its typical dreary, blustery fall weather. It's not exactly raining at the moment, but there's a fine mist floating down and everything is saturated through from the night's previous storm so that the air is thick with moisture. Everything feels damp and heavy. I huddle under the overhang to the left of the front doors and dial her number. As I place the phone to my ear, I turn the other direction to keep my back to the wind. Opposite me, on the right side of the front stairs, is a man in dark, over-sized clothing, smoking a cigarette. It's not uncommon to see passersby hovering by our front doors, with its large overhang that allows escape from the elements, but it's illegal for anyone to smoke within twenty-five feet of the building.

I bite my lip and wrap my arms tighter around my torso while listening to the phone ring. Should I say something to this man? I don't usually make a habit of talking to strangers. Besides, he's staring right at me with a speculative eye, one brow raised just slightly, as if he's gauging how I'll react. It's unnerving, so I hunch my shoulders and turn my back to him. The wind picks up and blows the fine drizzle directly in my face. *Hurry up and answer the damn phone, Terin!*

A click and then her sprightly voice follows. "It's about dang time, woman!"

"Yeah, well, I'm at work, and standing in the rain, and I don't have more than a few minutes so I can't talk long. The last thing I need is to give Gretta a reason to complain about me being on the phone during work hours. Why are you blowing up my phone today?"

"Ummm, hello? Because you haven't responded to the last four days of texts, so I figure if I'm annoying enough, you'll give in and answer. Are you okay?"

I sneak a quick glance over my shoulder to see if the man is still there. He is, but thankfully he's not looking at me. He's staring out into the street, still puffing on his cigarette as if in deep contemplation. As he brings it up to his mouth for another pull, I notice his last two fingers are black and blue, even the fingernails. Wincing, I wonder how he smashed them. The nails will eventually fall off.

I turn and huddle farther under the eave, out of the blowing wind. "Yeah, I'm totally fine. I've been busy, that's all. Is that the only reason you're harassing me? Just to make sure I'm okay?"

"Well, that, and I got VIP passes to that new bar downtown tomorrow night. I need you to go with me."

Icy wind swoops under my pant legs, sending goosebumps over my flesh. I scrunch my eyes tight.

23

I have no desire to go to a bar these days. "Eh, I don't know—"

She cuts me off. "No, don't you make any lame excuses. You've pouted around long enough. I know you keep saying you're fine but I know you, and I know when you're having a pity party. So, you're going to put on your big-girl panties and get the fuck over it. Got it?"

Before I can respond, she continues her speech. "Besides, I've been wanting to check out this new place since it opened last month. Now that I have VIP passes, I'm not missing out, and neither are you. You're my wingman. You're going."

Sigh. There's no point in arguing the issue. "Fine. How did you get VIP passes, anyway?"

"I won them on the radio," she says matter-of-factly, as if I should have known that information already.

We hang up. I pocket my phone and turn to retreat inside the building. Why on earth didn't I call her from the breakroom? Because I don't like my coworkers eavesdropping, that's why. And I was serious about not needing to give Gretta another reason to gripe at me. Sometimes I'm surprised she hasn't found some lame reason to fire me. I'm not even sure why she dislikes me so much.

The man is still there but he's staring at me again. I take in the details of his appearance. His hair is dirty blond, thin, and combed over strictly to the right. He's tall, maybe six feet two inches, and his frame is lean. His clothes are clean and neat, but he emanates a creepy vibe. His thin lips spread into a partial grin. I offer a brief smile and scurry toward the door.

"Excuse me, Miss?"

With my hand outstretched, grasping the door handle, I pause. "Yes?" I want to get inside where it's warm and dry.

"Can you tell me the best place to get a bite to eat? I'm new to the area and don't quite know my way around."

I point down the street, northbound. "Yeah, if you go two blocks down and turn left on Clover, you'll find an Irish pub. They serve breakfast all day and their hot sandwiches are delicious. Other than that, you won't find anything for another seven or eight blocks. Once you've made it that far, there's countless options."

His smile widens, revealing straight but slightly yellowed teeth. "Thanks. I appreciate it. Hey, do you work here? At the library?"

"Yes, I do."

"Do you live around here?"

Why is he asking me this? It seems an odd question to ask a stranger.

He waves his hand with a flick of the wrist. "Sorry. I'm not trying to pry. Just curious about the locals, you know. I'll see you around."

He turns and saunters down the stairs.

***

We're standing in line outside the front door of Club 530. I yank at the hem of my skirt as it clings to my bare thighs. "Whose idea was it to name the club after its address? Doesn't seem all that

25

creative, if you ask me."

Standing directly in front of me, gawking at the crowd ahead of us, Terin spins around. "Oh, quit your bitchin'. Who cares what they named the bar as long as they make stiff drinks, play good music, and we have a good time?" She reaches down and hikes my skirt back up another two inches. "And quit pulling this thing down. It's a mini-skirt. It's supposed to show some leg. And you have long, gorgeous legs, so show 'em off, girl. Rock it if you got it. That's what I say."

I clutch my handbag tighter to keep from pulling the skirt down. "I wish they'd let us in already. It's not exactly warm out here." Terin's brows furrow with disappointment. I quickly add, "But at least it's not raining." I really am being a Debbie Downer tonight. I need to knock it off and make the best of the evening. I'm here whether I like it or not.

"They'll let us in soon. We're in the VIP line. Hey, look at it this way, at least we're not in that line. They'll be out here for another hour at best."

I turn and scan the second line. She's not kidding. It spans the length of the sidewalk alongside the front of the building then wraps around the corner. My heart thuds in my chest when I spot a familiar face down by the corner, in the same line we're in.

Tom.

She must have seen him at the same time. "Crap. What is that asshole doing here?" Silent, I shrug, but keep my eyes fixed on him. He looks handsome, dressed in designer jeans and a button-up shirt, untucked. As if sensing me, he turns and locks

26

gazes. First, his expression is flat, unreadable. Then his strong features slowly melt into a toothy grin. That smile. My knees tremble. He's smiling at me. Without thinking, I smile back.

Stop. Texting. Me.

Those words slam into my brain and my smile fades as I relive that day in front of his home. I steer my gaze away and force myself to turn around. I refuse to look back in that direction.

Terin wraps an arm around my shoulders. "Don't let him get to you. Besides, you can do way better than him. He's too old for you. Just look at him, all dressed up looking like he's trying to be our age when we both know he's got at least a decade on us. Kind of creepy, if you ask me. Oh, hey! That reminds me." She grabs both my shoulders and her eyes widen as if she has suddenly remembered some juicy gossip. With Tom only about twenty yards behind me, I'm in no mood for trite banter.

"Did you hear on the news today that the authorities are saying they found the body of that woman who went missing a few months ago?"

I blink and stare stupidly into her face.

"Remember? Sheila Weaverton? The young gal up around the Bellingham area, the student who went missing late June, just before finals?"

I shake my head, finally catching up with the sudden change in conversation. "Yeah. Of course I remember her. She's the one they found that snuff film on. They were still looking for the body last I knew. How could I forget? The whole country knows. That stuff is frightening. Gives me the heebie-jeebies. Wait. Why are we talking about this? They found her?"

Terin's expression is mixed with fascination and horror. "Yeah, they found her just outside of Blaine, down by a river right before the Canadian border. I can't even think of that whole thing without getting the chills. I mean, can you imagine what that woman went through? And can you believe there's people in this world who watch stuff like that? What in the hell is wrong with people?"

I suppress a shiver. "I don't know. When it leaked on the internet it disgusted me how many people immediately watched it. Granted, they pulled the video pretty quickly, so it was only up for a day, but still, why...how...could anyone want to see some woman murdered for entertainment? It's just like when people watch beheadings from the Middle East. I don't get it."

Terin shakes her head. Her face pales even under the streetlights. "I had never even heard of a snuff film until all this happened."

"Me either." A wave of anxiety washes over me. This story. This night. Everything, has me on edge. I don't even want to be here. "Hey, can we change the subject? I don't want to think about any of that right now. I don't really want to think of anything, to be honest."

Terin closes her eyes and gives one quick shake of the head. When she opens her eyes again she's smiling. "You're totally right! We're here to shake off the week and have a good time. Right?"

I nod. "Right." The conversation has left me raw and uncomfortable in my own skin. My dress suddenly feels too revealing. I shouldn't be here. I think of Tom standing behind me and it takes everything I have not to steal another glance in his direction. Finally, the doors open and our line slowly files inside.

Music pumps in bellowing waves that reverberate throughout my body. Too loud. Much louder than it needs to be. People stand around in small cliques, waiting for the next flirtation, the next heartache. My thoughts are toxic. I chew on a fingernail and contemplate excuses to leave.

"Tessa?"

I recognize Gerald's voice from behind me, and by the look on Terin's face, I see that I'm right. I give her the *I can't believe this crap* look before I turn and offer him a plastic smile. "Hey, how are you?"

He's dressed in a polo shirt and jeans, and actually looks almost handsome but a little out of place in this environment. "I'm good. Just checking out the new place. One of my friends works here and got me in early. Cool, right?"

I nod my head, glancing around. For some reason, I'm terrified that Tom will see me talking with Gerald. "Yeah, pretty cool." I don't know what else to say so I stand there looking like an idiot.

Terin grabs me by the elbow. "Hey, Gerald. Good to see you. I'm gonna steer this girl toward the bar, but maybe we'll catch up with ya later." Without waiting, she puts pressure on my arm and actually steers me away from Gerald, just as she said.

Gerald frowns. "Oh, okay, but maybe I'll buy you a drink later. Huh?"

29

I glance over my shoulder, raising my voice over the music. "Later. Yeah, later."

I turn and we scurry away. "Oh, thank God. I owe you, Terin. You saved the day back there."

She smirks smugly. "Yeah, yeah, what's new?"

I pause. "Wait, no. That's not right. I don't owe you. This is your fault. I shouldn't be here. It seems anyone and everyone I don't want to see tonight is right here in this damn bar. I mean, what are the chances of that?"

The flat look on her face tells me she doesn't give a damn.

"Never mind." I lure her to the bar. "I need a drink. Now."

"'Atta girl. Here, I'll get the first round."

She aggressively pushes past a small group of young, lascivious women. They're giggling and tossing their hair around. Even in this dark atmosphere I see their thick makeup and recognize their pathetic desperation. Is this what I look like? Self-conscious, I yank my skirt down. She orders two Adios Motherfuckers. We'll be drunk in no time. I'm shooting for a mix of numb and fearless.

While the bartender mixes our drinks, I glance down the length of the bar. At the far end, another face stands out among the crowd. I blink repeatedly, trying to place it. Half a minute passes as I scroll through my memory bank. That's it. The man in front of the library the day before, the smoker. He's staring at me. Another man stands next to him, his attention focused on one of the other bartenders. A chill runs up my spine. He smiles but I don't smile back this time. I turn toward Terin just as she hands over my drink. There is an odd feeling to the evening already. Terin was right, this bar is the hottest new thing on this end of town.

"Bottoms up." She takes a long pull of the blue concoction through her straw. I follow suit. Tequila overpowers all other flavors, even the blue curacao. Tequila, take me away.

A little while later, my lips tingle nicely and the perfect amount of *I don't care* ensconces my body. Stress and shame melt away. My best friend drags me to the dance floor and I let her. My hair feels longer than usual since I straightened it for the evening. I feel it swing below my shoulder blades while we sway and gyrate to the beat. I feel almost sexy...an unusual feeling for me.

I sense him seconds before he places a hand on my shoulder. I turn and look up into Tom's face. He's smiling down like a Cheshire cat. I blink, then give in and flash him a quick smile, while keeping up with the pumping music, though I'm utterly confused. He leans down to my ear and yells, "I'm surprised to see you here."

I shrug.

His hand snakes out and touches the ends of my hair. "I always liked your hair like this. Straight and silky, rather than your unruly curls. Gives you more of a sophisticated look. You look stunning."

His attempt at a compliment offends me. I've always been a little sensitive about my naturally curly auburn hair. Over the years I've learned to appreciate it. They're easy to work with, not kinky or anything like that. But still, I get a little defensive about them.

31

Terin spins me around. "You want me to get rid of him?"

I should probably say yes. I should definitely say yes. "No. It's okay. He's not hurting anything." I suck down the last of my drink.

"It's okay," Tom says. "I was just saying hi anyway. We'll chat again later." He offers a devilish smile with full eye contact before he walks away.

I take a deep breath. Gain composure. "Hey, I'm going to get us another round. Stay here."

Without looking back, I stroll off the dance floor and head to the bar. Tom's behavior confuses me. He shoved me out of his life and now he's flirting with me like nothing happened. Pressing up against the tall wood frame of the bar, I order two of the same. Seconds later, Tom sneaks up next to me and presses his hip to mine. I recognize his form instantly. Heat rises from my toes to my brain. It's way too hot in here.

He doesn't look at me until after he orders a scotch. Then he gently places a warm hand to the small of my back and leans down. His lips graze my ear, sending shivers up my spine. I want to lean into him but I don't.

"I've missed you. Save me a dance later." He pulls away and pays the bartender before walking away. Sleek. Very sleek. I hate him. I hate myself more for wanting to dance with him.

Less than an hour later, I'm dizzy and sweaty. I feel…elated because I'm actually having fun. To be honest, I'm high on anticipation, waiting for that dance with Tom. Terin has wandered off to the restroom and I suspect she may actually be making out in a corner somewhere with the guy she's been bumping and grinding with since we got here. A little breathless, I decide to sit out the next song and meander to the side of the room, away from the dance floor. Thankfully, I have not seen Gerald again.

Tom intervenes from out of nowhere, wrapping an arm around my waist and steering me toward the back door. Senses skewed, I'm slow to react. My head swoons as I tip my chin up. "Where are we g-going?" I slur.

"Thought you might need some fresh air." His voice is smooth and comforting but his face blurs in and out of focus. I wish I hadn't had that third drink. It's not until we're out in the back alley that I try to pull myself together. The fresh, cold air pricks my skin and helps clear my senses. A little.

He pulls me around the corner and pushes me against the cold, brick wall. His lips are on mine, his tongue pushes through and dances across my teeth. I part my mouth and he kisses me desperately. I drink him up. Does he still have feelings for me? Maybe he regrets pushing me out of his life so harshly.

One hand gropes my right breast, the other hand slides up under my skirt. I've never let a man kiss me like this out in public. I kind of like it but I feel self-conscious too.

"Tom, wait. Someone will see," I say between kisses.

He pulls back, looks left, then right down the alleyway. "Come on, then. My car is right around

33

the corner." Without waiting for a response, he bolts to the right, dragging me along behind. Things are happening too fast. I want to clear my head. But it all feels so good too.

As we approach his BMW, he reaches into his jeans pocket, whips out the keys, and hits the unlock button. Instead of opening the front passenger door, he opens the back door. "Get in."

I hesitate. A flash of anger passes over his features. I don't want to upset him, so I quickly slide into the backseat. Tom sinks into the seat next to me and slams the door behind him. His lips crush over mine once again. His hand runs up my right calf to my knee, and then up the inside of my inner thigh. Butterflies flutter low in my abdomen. I want this but I don't know what it means. Tom broke up with me a week ago, and it wasn't even a gentle breakup. It was brutal. My thoughts are muddled. His fingers slip under my panties and slide inside me. A guttural gasp escapes my lips and my hips thrust upward to allow him in further. My body is not my own.

His lips stray down my neck, trailing wet kisses. "Yes, sweet Tess. I've not seen this side of you. I like it."

I'm not sure I like it. My back arches and I tip my head back as he explores my body. The world is spinning and I'm beginning to feel sick to my stomach. My ears ring loudly. Sensations, good and bad, mix inextricably.

Then his hand is on the back of my head, shoving me down. What is happening? He fumbles for his zipper, then his cock juts out. His fingers twist in my hair, pulling at the roots, and tears spring to my eyes. Before I can complain, he shoves me down, and without thinking I open my mouth to take him in. Up and down, he guides my rhythm until he is pumping harder and harder into my mouth. Tears slide down my cheeks. This is not what I want to be doing. Bile rises into my throat and I gag.

His grip tightens in my hair and his hips pause briefly. "Don't you dare throw up." He gives my head a little shake. I cry out.

"Do you hear me?"

I nod my head but I'm sobbing uncontrollably. I can't see anything but his lap and the floorboard because he still has my head held tightly in his grasp.

"Good. Now, you can't just leave me like this. You got me all worked up. You gotta finish what you started."

Pain spreads across the back of my skull as he twists a little tighter to guide me back to where he wants me. Like a good girl, I open wide and let him abuse my mouth until he is finished. My eyes squeeze tight as I focus on not puking. I'm trying not to think, but relentless, ugly thoughts crop up anyway. How did I get here? Why is he doing this? This is what I get for being a stupid girl.

Gag. Breathe in. Breathe out.

His legs tense up. He's getting close.

He never treated me like this before. He wasn't exactly sweet, but he was never like this. Or was he and I was just too blind to see it? I'm so stupid.

His legs stiffen, his hips thrust higher while he

35

clenches his buttocks. His grip tightens unforgivingly in my hair. Warm, salty, thick liquid spurts into my mouth. As soon as his body begins to relax, I sit up and slide back as far away from him as I can get, pressing my back against the opposite door. I wipe my mouth and gag.

"Why? What's wrong with you? You didn't have to be so rough," I cry.

His expression is a mix of mild amusement and disgust as he zips up his pants, then reaches across my body, and with a flick of the wrist opens the door. "Get out."

I'm stunned. He's acting as if I'm the one who committed an offense.

"Stop staring at me with that stupid Tessa blank stare. I said, get the fuck out of my car."

Something more insidious than guilt or embarrassment engulfs me. I've felt both of those frequently in my life. This is shame all the way to my core. I'm crying so hard now I can hardly make out the features of his face. Scrambling like a rag doll, I stagger out of the car and nearly fall on my face when my left ankle turns inward, just like it did in front of his home the week before. I stumble and catch myself. Beyond humiliated, I want nothing more than to hide. As soon as I'm upright, I break into a run. I'm in heels, so I stagger-step multiple times, but I'm determined to get anywhere but right here.

Blindly, I run across the lot. As I round the corner, I run smack into someone as they are coming the opposite direction.

"Tessa? Are you okay?"

I glance up through the stream of tears to see a blurry image of Gerald. "No, no. I just want to go home." I push off his chest and stumble backward, then turn and flee the opposite direction without saying a word, ignoring Gerald's plea of confusion as the distance between us widens. I pray he won't follow. I just want to get away from this place.

I keep running until I'm at least a few blocks away. Winded, fatigued, and little sick to my stomach, I stop. I lean against the wall of a building, taking in sharp gasps of air, and look around. Thankfully, Gerald didn't follow. Where am I? Terin. I left Terin back at the club. I can't go back there. I'll have to call her and let her know I've gone home. She'll be fine.

My phone? Where is my phone? It was in my handbag. I had my handbag when I left the club with Tom. *Shit.* It must be in his car. Fear, pain, shame, anger, guilt, all well up tight within my chest and rise until I feel as if I will go mad. I run my fingers through my hair and cry so hard I start to gag again. I want to puke. *Get that man out of me. Get him out!*

"Can I help you? Are you okay?"

Startled, I spin around. The man from the library is standing at the corner, maybe fifteen feet away. My crying wanes as muddled thoughts spin around in my mind, trying to make sense of it all. Why is he here? Did he follow me from the club? His brow is pinched with a look of concern. He takes a step forward. "Are you okay?"

My knees and hands are trembling violently. "I'm…I'm fine." I drag both hands across my face, swiping away the tears.

He takes another step forward. "Are you sure? You seem upset. Are you ill?"

I take a step back. I don't want any further interaction tonight. I've had more than enough. All I want to do is go home. And this guy…he seems friendly, but he freaks me out. "No, really. I'm fine. I'm just on my way home."

Another step forward. "Do you need a ride?"

Another step back. Why won't anyone listen to me? "No. I'm fi…"

Something is pulled over my head from behind. The world is dark and muffled. I scream. Hands go around my waist. My arms arc outward, side to side, hoping to hit anything in my path. What is happening? Fear, stark and white, drains the blood from my head to my toes. I'm dizzy.

Voices bark out sharp orders but I'm flailing about and screaming so I can't make out what they're saying. Another set of hands grab my legs and pull them out from under me so now I'm being carried by two men…one by my waist and the other by my legs. I writhe and twist. I have to get out of this. I need to get away. What is happening? My breath plumes in and out in short, hot gasps inside the small bag over my head. Claustrophobia flares up. A stronger wave of panic follows. I'm…going…to pass…out.

CHAPTER THREE

Eyes open. Darkness. Eyes close. Darkness. Where am I? I can't breathe. I'm so hot. Memory floods back. Eyes open wide. The bag is still over my head. My heart thuds in my chest and my respirations increase. The humidity of my warm breath presses against my face. I really can't breathe. Instead of flailing around, I hold still and hone in on my other senses. I'm sitting upright, and by the way my body bounces in the seat, I know I'm in a vehicle of some sort and the road is not paved. It's rough. Over the sound of my desperate panting, I make out the hum of the engine and crunch of tires against rugged terrain.

Oh god! Oh god! Oh god! Where are they taking me?

"Slow down, Jake. We're bumping around like crazy back here."

I snap my head toward the left, following the sound of the man's voice. Is it the man from the library or the other one who grabbed me from behind? Racking my brain, I think back to what his voice sounded like. I think the man next to me is the one from the library. He was in the club tonight too. So the driver must be Jake. How many are there?

"Hold tight! I just want to get there already," a man barks from the front. His tone is much sharper, deeper. Dangerous. I'm not okay, I'm not okay. Fuck. *Breathe in. Breathe out. Breathe in.* Too fast. I'm breathing too fast. It's too damn hot in this bag. My back and hips ache as I'm jostled about. The taste and smell of stale tequila wafts into my warm nostrils. A thick wave of nausea suddenly rises. Oh, no, I'm going to throw up. Not in the bag. I'll choke. I can't hold it down.

Sour, vile fluid bubbles up and bursts from my mouth and nose. I gag and retch inside the sack. Feels like I'm inside a microwave that has cooked too long and burst the contents. Vomit spews over my lips and down my face and neck, pooling up at the neck where the bag is cinched tight.

"Oh, shit, Jake. She's fucking puking. Pull over."

"I'm not pulling over," Jake yells. "We aren't far enough out of town."

I'm trying to breathe but my nose and mouth are full of rancid phlegm. There's no oxygen. Instinct has me groping at the bottom of the bag, scratching and pulling to get it off. Thank god my hands are free. My feet kick out and make contact with the seat in front of me. Pain sears up the front of my shins, but I keep writhing and pulling.

"No, seriously, man. Pull over. She's freaking out."

"I don't care. We don't have our masks on. She'll see our faces."

40

"She's already seen my face, dumbass," the other man yells. "Who freaking cares? It's not like she'll be able to identify us when we're done with her anyway. I've got to do something or she's going to choke on her own fluids and then this whole thing will be a damn waste. Can't you hear her choking?"

"Well, then, take the damn bag off her head, Vance. Shit, I can't do everything. I'm driving. Figure it out!"

Hands join mine and clamber to undo the ties. "Just sit still a second. Hold on," he demands.

Desperate to get out of the bag and take a breath, I stop yanking on the ties. But I can't stop gagging. I'm covered in vomit and fear. The bonds around my neck loosen and the material is pulled up over my face, then off of my head in a rush. A wave of cool, fresh air hits my face. Big, deep breath. Another. And another.

Blink. Wipe puke from my nose and mouth. Turn to my right. The man from the library stares at me, wide-eyed. Then the smell hits him and his nose puckers. He draws his hands to his nose and covers it, flinching away from me. I spot the bruised fingernails that have yet to heal and shiver.

I take a quick glance at the driver, Jake. Facing front, his shoulders hunched forward, all I know is that he is large, formidable. I'm not sure about his height, but his build is thick and gnarly, like a body builder. His hands are strong, and maneuver the car with ease over the rough dirt road. It's dark outside, and I cannot see anything more than what the headlights shine upon within twenty feet of the front of the...SUV, yes, looks like an SUV of some sort.

41

Maybe a Jeep or an Explorer. I need to get out of this damn car.

Turning toward the right passenger door, I scramble for the handle. My hands are slick with my own bodily fluids. I can't get a good grip. When I finally wrap my fingers around the handle, I fervently jiggle it back and forth, but it's locked. The tight sensation in my ribcage cinches tighter.

"Jesus, Vance," Jake bellows out. "Why aren't her hands tied?" He reaches back with one arm still on the steering wheel, the other swinging out to grab hold of me before I escape. His strong fingers bite into my upper arm. My hands shake violently, and they seem to have a mind of their own as I search for the unlock button. My fingers flitter about inside the dark car, searching desperately for the automatic locks.

Another set of hands grip my waist as Vance jerks me back toward the middle of the seat. High pitched, breathy sounds squeak from my wet lips as I bend at the waist and strain forward, still trying to make contact with the locking mechanism. Where in the hell is it?

The hand around my arm loosens, then quickly finds my hair and jerks back hard. My chin juts straight up in the air so that I'm staring at the dark ceiling. Searing pain shoots down the back side of my neck, as well as at the roots of my hair. Tears blur my vision. Still, my hands continue to clamber blindly at the door. I need to get out. *I need out!*

"Dammit, hold still." Vance wraps an arm tighter around my waist while the other snakes around to rein in my arms. Without thinking about it, I jerk

42

my left elbow back and connect with his jaw.

"Shit," he whispers through clenched teeth. "Stop flailing around, dammit. Just stop." Both arms reach up and wrestle for mine.

"That's it," Jake yells, releasing my hair. Suddenly the car slams to a stop. Tires slide against gravel. My head tips forward, and my vision tunnels. Vance's grasp loosens. With my head free, I twist toward him and aim my flailing arms in his direction. Hitting him over and over again, connecting with cheek, arms, chin, chest, anything I can that might possibly cause him enough pain to release me. I need to hurry. Jake is now out of the driver's-side door and rounding the front of the vehicle. I'm screaming. The sound escapes from deep within my diaphragm and rattles my bones, echoing within the confines of the vehicle. Desperation seizes my senses. Time slows, as if I'm stuck in a bad dream. Maybe I am. But the pain shooting up my arms as I hit and punch tell me this is all too real.

Vance blocks my blows, trying to protect his face while simultaneously attempting to seize my arms again. The door behind me swings open. Hands, stronger and larger than Vance's, grip my waist and haul me out of the vehicle. Fingers bite into my flesh. Frantic, I kick and thrash every limb I have. I arch my back, hoping to somehow wriggle out of his grip. No chance. He's too strong.

He sets my feet on the ground, then wraps one muscled bicep around my throat. Instantly, I lose the ability to pull oxygen into my airway. I kick my feet back, connecting with his shins. I claw and

43

scratch at the bulk of muscle around my neck. His skin curls under my fingernails. Stars dance before my eyes. First, tiny white bursts, they quickly morph into frightening red blotches.

Breathe in.

No air will pass.

I'm...going...again. Please...help...

CHAPTER FOUR

Before consciousness fully embraces me, I'm already remembering the evening's events. A nightmare that is not really a nightmare at all. My eyelids feel heavy, reluctant to open as white, hot pain shoots through my head. My throat hurts. I'm lying uncomfortably on my right side, my head tipped awkwardly without a pillow under me. A kink in my neck spasms, starting behind my right ear, traveling to my shoulder. Both shoulders burn from the strain of the position I'm in, my wrists bound firmly behind my back. Lower lip trembles. I don't want to open my eyes.

Please, God, just let it all be a bad dream. A nightmare.

The smell of stale urine combines with something cooking, assaulting my nostrils. Bacon? Seems an odd scent, given my scenario. My stomach roils from the rich aroma. Food is the last thing I can think of. I still feel queasy and weak. More from the blow to my head than the alcohol.

Slowly, slowly, blink, blink. My eyes are gritty

45

and dry. The room I'm in comes into focus, then blurs, then focuses again. The door straight ahead is worn wood. It's closed. The walls are wood also, adding a rustic feel to the place...like an old, abandoned cabin. Though I cannot see the rest of it, I sense its compact size pressing in on me.

The smell of urine wafts up from the twin-sized bed I'm lying on. Without sheets, I can see it's one of those old striped mattresses. It sinks deeply in the middle. I arch my head back to take in the rest of my surroundings and my neck instantly spasms again. The room is empty. Like, really empty. Stark. Nothing but the bed I'm on and me. I'm alone. This gives me a brief moment of comfort.

Think. I need to think. I'm in the second location. This is bad. Really fucking bad. I remember watching an *Oprah* episode where they gave tips on how to survive a kidnapping. The number one tip was to never let your kidnapper take you to "the second location." You're too vulnerable there. That's where they will likely kill you. My heart skips and gallops faster.

Breathe in. Breathe out. Calm down.

I'm not going to die. Not today.

Fuck, why am I so stupid? How could I have let this happen? I'm sickened by the fact that I'm crying again, hot tears sliding sideways down my face, rather than coming up with a plan.

Okay, okay, okay. I can do this.

I try to sit up, but without the use of my hands, I end up flopping around on the bed like a fish. Every inch of my body aches. Finally, I swing my legs over the side of the bed, kick out my left leg, and use the momentum for leverage while using my stomach muscles to sit up with a heave. The bed springs squeak and complain below me. The room spins for a few moments, then settles. I take a deep, calming breath and look around the room again. There's an overhead light but it's off, and I wonder if this rundown cabin of sorts even has electricity.

Thin, grayish light filters in through a dirty window to the left of the room. It's morning. Early, and gloomy with a thick layer of clouds. I'm guessing maybe between six and seven a.m. Somehow, probably due to being knocked over the head and choked, I slept for at least four or five hours. I'm not sure exactly how late it was when I left the club. After midnight, I know that.

I shiver and goosebumps spread over the surface of my skin. It's cold and damp. It doesn't help that I'm only wearing a sleeveless satin shirt and my miniskirt. The hem is hiked up all the way to my hipbones, revealing thin, lacy panties. I want to pull it down but there is absolutely no give in the ropes binding my wrists. I don't bother straining against them. My feet are cold and bare. Where are my shoes?

Something out of the corner of my eye catches my attention. I twist my torso to look in the corner behind me. There is something else in the room. A camera mounted on a tripod. Its red light blinks conspiratorially at me. I swallow down the lump of fear that rises in my throat. I'm being videotaped? Watched? I stand, then take a quick step back to catch myself as my wobbly knees give out. I regain my footing, then walk to the camera, my gait unsteady at first. I'm careful to be quiet so as not to draw attention to myself. A foot before I reach the camera, my body lurches to a stop as the bonds on my wrists strain to their limit. I spin around and glare at my leash. Like a dog, I'm tied to the bare, stripped-down bed.

Still curious about the camera, I resume my inspection. My distorted reflection stares back at me in the dark lens. I barely recognize the woman staring back at me. A shiver runs down my spine. My body trembles. I'm in so much trouble.

The door swings open behind me and I spin around. A whoosh of air enters the room with the smell of bacon riding it. The bulky one, Jake, looms in the doorway with one hand on the doorknob.

"You're awake. Good. Step away from the camera, though. That's rule number one. Don't. Touch. The camera. Understood?"

He's speaking to me with calm precision, as if we're having a simple conversation about something as trite as the weather. But we aren't. He's my kidnapper and he's giving me the rules. That's good, though, right? I mean, if there are rules, it means I'll be around for a while. He doesn't plan to kill me, at least not right away. I take solace in that thought.

As he shuts the door behind him, I glance over his shoulder. The room behind him is small, all wood walls too. There's a lantern on a picnic-type table. On the other side of the table is a small sink and a kerosene cook stove, like something you'd take camping, propped on the counter. Very rough living situation. Dank, abandoned. A musty smell lingers under the scent of bacon.

The only thought that runs over and over in my head is that no one will ever find me out here. This is terror. I wonder where Vance is. He seems to be the gentler of the two, if there is such a thing.

I try to take a step back but again my restraints keep me rooted in place.

Jake puts both hands up as if showing me he's harmless. "Hey, hey. Don't freak out again. I just came in here to see if you're hungry? That's all. You want something to eat?" His voice is low and calm, as if speaking to a frightened animal he wants to coax out of hiding. But there is a malignant threat beneath the façade.

He wants to offer me food? I shake my head. Food is the last thing I want right now. The reek of vomit permeates my hair. I can't bear to talk to this man, much less take food from him.

He takes a few steps forward, bends down, and grabs hold of the ropes that bind my wrists. With a mischievous grin on his face, he looks at the camera, then back at me. "Come here."

Unsure of how to navigate this precarious situation, I don't move at all.

His lips twitch and his left brow raises. Then with one sharp motion, he jerks the rope. Skin under the ropes burn and peel away as my body spins and lurches forward. In an attempt to catch my balance before falling on my face, I do a clumsy sideways stagger-step and recover just inches in front of him.

Standing closer than I want to be, I can't stop my muscles from trembling. He sneers down at me. His teeth are crooked. His jaw is wide. His skin is covered in acne, and I'm sure he takes steroids on a regular basis to gain his bulk. His scent is heavy with sweat. It mixes inextricably with the smell of frying pork.

He holds a finger in front of his face in warning. "Do not play with me, little girl." He gives the rope another jerk. "Do you understand me?"

"Y-y-yes," I whimper.

"Good. Now let me explain a few things. You see that camera over there?"

When I don't take my gaze from his to look toward the camera, he moves faster than I can react and clutches my chin in his large hand, his thumb and forefinger digging into the flesh of my jaw. My lips pucker out. He jerks my head to the right so that I'm facing the camera. He points to it with his other hand. "There. Do you see it now?"

Face still in his grasp, I nod adamantly to show I'm listening now. This man is frightening beyond measure.

His thumb and fingers squeeze harder. "Good. That camera will watch you day and night. You hear me?"

I nod, unable to suppress the incessant whimpering that bubbles from my core.

"You will not go near it. You will do as you're told. Or I will hurt you. You got it?"

I nod.

He releases my chin and slaps me across the face. My head snaps hard to the left and my right cheek flashes hot where his palm connected. Instant tears stream down my face. He grabs my chin again and hauls me upright.

"Answer me when I ask you a question. Understand?"

"Yes, yes."

"You and that camera right there are going to make me a lot of money. Do you understand?"

I don't understand at all. I'm afraid to. "Yes." I nod over and over again. "Yes."

"Good. Now sit your ass down."

Before I can do as I'm told, he gives me a shove. I topple onto the bed. Unable to catch myself with my hands behind my back, I fall to my side, then scramble to sit upright.

He gives me a look of disgust before walking out the door and slamming it behind him.

Defeated and scared beyond words, I'm paralyzed. I need to escape, but I fear this man's wrath if he catches me. I bite my lip and earnestly try to fight back the tears. But they are relentless and gush forth anyway. I give in and let them come. Racking sobs engulf my body. I look toward the camera, no longer innocuous. It stares at me menacingly, my only witness.

What will it see?

CHAPTER FIVE

Pace. Pace. Pace back and forth alongside the bed, as far as my leash will allow. Steal glances at my witness staring back at me from the corner of the room. I can't decide whether to think of the object as an enemy, watching silently, passively. Or as an ally, quietly capturing my plight, possibly something I can use to benefit me. But how?

I come to an abrupt halt as memories of a conversation from the night before plummet through the center of my frazzled brain. Terin and I, standing out in front of the club. We talked about the girl from Bellingham. What was her name? Sheila something. Weaverton, I think. She'd been kidnapped months ago. Murdered. Everything captured on camera solely for the purpose of being sold on the black market. A heinous, revolting crime.

A snuff film.

I can't feel my face. My lips and fingers buzz sharply. With shaky, unstable limbs, I plop down on the edge of the bed before I pass out. I'm the next

Sheila Weaverton. I'm not sure how I know, but I do.

My cell phone. I left my cellphone behind, in my handbag. I'm certain it's in Tom's car. The events in his backseat bring hot humiliation to my cheeks. I close my eyes, reliving the entire evening in a single flash. If I had just been less pathetic. If only I had stayed in the bar, away from Tom. Better yet, if I had just stayed home in the first place. Terin said it so perfectly, I need to stick up for myself. I need to stand my ground. She probably didn't mean against her, but if I had merely said, "No, I don't want to go to the club," I wouldn't be where I am now.

God, poor Terin. She's probably worried sick about me. She's probably called my phone a thousand times. Would Tom answer it? Would he try to drop it by my place? Someone, somehow would eventually discover I'm missing, right? Agh! I want to scream.

Opening my eyes, I force myself back into the now. There's no use in lingering in the past. My life depends on having only productive, focused thoughts that will get me out of this predicament. *Predicament.* I almost laugh. The word seems much too innocuous for the peril I'm in.

A door slams and two tenor voices fill the empty walls of the cabin on the other side of my bedroom wall. Vance has returned. From where, though? Can he come and go as he pleases? Does that mean we aren't too far out of town? I wish I had been able to see where we were going. I'm not even sure how long it took us to get here because I had been in and out of consciousness.

Straining to decipher the conversation, my muscles freeze in place so as not to cause any extraneous noise. My breathing shallows.

"Yeah, she's awake." Jake's voice is gruff and muffled. I imagine him stuffing food into his mouth while relaying recent events to Vance.

"Well, how is she?"

"She fucking stinks. That's how she is. Smells like puke. You're going to help me give her a bath in a minute here. Just as soon as I'm done eating. You want some food?"

"No, I had something already." Vance's tone is no less gruff, but for some reason I find it less menacing. Maybe because he has yet to hurt me. This is ridiculous, of course. He's the one who had been following me in the first place. I shake my head.

"How do you intend to bathe her? There's not even a bathroom in this place."

A chair scrapes against the floor. Dishes clink in the sink. Jake is done with his meal. "I'll show you."

Muscles freeze tighter. I clasp my hands together behind me, my palms sweaty and my wrists stinging. Staring at the bedroom door, I wait in dread for my captors to enter.

"Wait," Vance shouts as Jake strolls through the bedroom door. "You're not wearing a mask. What about the camera?"

Jake's tone and body language show his growing agitation as he turns to face Vance. "Dude, I'm not wearing that damn ski mask for this one. That thing was a pain in the ass last time. Felt like I couldn't

54

breathe. I couldn't see worth a damn and that chick kept grabbing at it every chance she got. Way more trouble than it's worth."

"So you're just going to be identifiable to anyone who watches it?"

Jake shakes his head in disbelief. "No. Are you stupid? I'm going to blur out our faces when I edit the tape, dumbass. By the time I'm done with it, no one will be able to tell us from their own neighbor. Jesus, you think I'm some kind of idiot or something?"

Vance looks apprehensive and holds back when Jake approaches me. As if sensing what he wants, I stand up just before he reaches the bed. Crouching low, he reaches under the metal frame and unties my leash. "Grab the camera, Vance."

Abandoning any lingering hesitation, Vance leaps into action and lifts the camera off the tripod. Holding it out in front, pointed my direction, he faces us. Jake stands tall and gathers the rope until there is very little slack between the two of us. "Follow me."

Jake turns swiftly and marches forward. Even though I leap forward to keep up, the rope pulls taut against my wrists. Searing pain shoots up my forearms. My bare feet scuff along the dirty floor as I rush to keep up. I'm getting a bath despite lacking a bathroom and I dread whatever that means.

My skirt rides up so I can feel my butt hanging out, and all I can think about is Vance following behind with the camera. Mortified, my cheeks flush hot, but I keep my focus in front of me so I can anticipate Jake's next moves.

We file through the bedroom door and into the living space, which serves as a compact kitchen and living room, with a miniature television in the corner and one pea green couch along the wall. The cabin is dilapidated and grimy, but it has a lived-in feel to it. I wonder if one of these men actually lives here. It's too small for both of them.

Distracted, I trip and stumble over a broken board in the flooring. My body propels forward faster than my feet can keep up with. My arms strain against my bindings in an attempt to brace against the fall. Jarring pain shoots from knee to hip when my right knee slams against the floor. Without arms to protect my face, my chin crashes against the dusty floor seconds later. Teeth collide together. My brain jostles within my skull.

Hair falls over my face, blinding me. I spurt and sputter the dust from my dry mouth, rolling over to my back, my wrists pressed painfully into the floor under me. Jake looms directly above, staring down at with me with impatience. With a violent tug, he barks at me. "Get up."

The force drags me a foot toward him across the dirty flooring. Vance stands two feet away, camera in hand, a quiet spectator. I roll back to my stomach and try to bring my knees up under me so I can stand. Jake stomps toward me. His fingers lace through the hair at the nape of my neck and brings me to my feet with a sharp pull. I scream, tears streaming down my cheeks as a headache spreads from the bottom of my skull to the crown of my head. "Stop, stop. That hurts," I yelp.

Jake doesn't care. Vance doesn't care.

Jake lets go of my hair and spins toward the door, dragging me along as if nothing happened. He jerks the front door open and we exit the cabin. Fresh air welcomes my nose but assaults my skin. Goosebumps prickle up over every inch of my body. Fall has brought brisk temperatures to the Northwest. The ground is damp. The sky is an unbroken slate of gray.

I scan the grounds. We are at the end of a rugged dirt road. Tall grass grows wildly along the tire tracks. Evergreens and birch trees cluster thickly, encircling the property. Silence permeates our surroundings. Even the birds hide out today. The isolation fills me with dread.

I scurry down the two battered steps. Mud seeps between my toes when we reach the bottom. Shivers contract my tired muscles. I'm whimpering, snot and tears smearing down my face in a sticky mess.

Jake leads us along the front of the shack and around the corner, down a short path. He stops suddenly and snatches a hose off the ground. With a flick of the wrist, he twists the round knob to turn it on. Rusty pipes moan and complain before water coughs and spurts through the line. It strikes me odd that the house has running water but no bathroom.

Before I can ponder this further, Jake yanks me closer and holds the hose over my head. Icy water cascades over my scalp, into my hair, and spills down my body. A shrill cry escapes my lips. I twist and dance without thinking about my actions, writhing to get away. Jake laughs and latches onto a lock of wet hair, making sure I stay directly under the stream of water. I can't see. Water drips down into my eyes. I blink over and over again. I gasp for breath. Jake redirects the water straight into my face. I sputter and gasp for air as cold liquid fills my open mouth and nose. Oxygen. I need oxygen. Shivering uncontrollably, my muscles cramp and quiver.

Jake drops my leash to the ground. With one hand holding the hose, the other tugs on my skirt. He pulls it over my hips and down my legs in one swoop. The shirt follows, so that I'm standing in only my bra and panties. Shivering. His hand returns to scrub my hair. Gasp for air. I'm so cold.

He gropes along the curves of my body, his calloused hand scratching along the surface of my skin like a rough luffa. The hose follows, away from my face, finally allowing me to breathe in a full, clean breath. When my eyes clear, I catch Vance out of the corner of my vision. Watching and recording everything. Humiliation consumes me. This cannot be happening. I want to fight but my muscles are screaming. Fatigue plagues me. I'm sure I must have a severe concussion by the way it takes everything to stand upright rather than fall to my knees.

Give up, I think while I shiver and shake and sob under the frigid water. I tip my head back and gape up at the blank, stark sky, and for the briefest of moments I silently beg for answers. Why? Why is this happening to me? What have I done to deserve this? I've never felt so bare, so naked, so exposed, so alone, in my life.

No one answers. No one hears me. I am alone.

58

CHAPTER SIX

Cold to the bone, I march in silence behind Jake. Vance follows quietly.

I'm numb. Cold...but somehow numb at the same time. I'm outside of my body watching from a distance now. It's as if I'm watching a movie. Just as hundreds, maybe thousands, of disturbed souls will do when they watch this film. When I'm already dead. Forgotten. No longer a real human being. Just someone to gossip about, feel sympathy for.

Down the muddy path. Up the two rickety stairs. Through the door. Heat embraces my body as we enter the cabin and leave the cool fall weather outside. This time, when I smell remnants of bacon, my stomach reacts with interest. I haven't eaten since early evening the day before.

Through the small living space and back to the bedroom. No one has said a word since the hose was turned off. Jake crouches low and reties me to the bedframe. The only sound is the chattering of my teeth. I look down at my muddy feet and notice my toes have a bluish tinge. I imagine my hands and lips look similar. I shiver so hard it looks as if I'm having a mild seizure. If only my hands were free so I could rub them up and down my arms and legs for friction. Any heat at all would be welcome.

When Jake stands to his full height, he seems tired too. Either that, or he's bored. I wonder if he slept at all last night. His gaze shifts to Vance, then back to me. He glances down at his clothing. "Shit, I'm all wet." His brow furrows but his tone remains flat. "Look what you did. Now I have to change." Without another word, he stomps out of the room. His moods baffle me.

Vance hovers in the corner of the room, returning the camera to its tripod home. When he turns, I feel the weight of his stare. Standing awkwardly next to the bed, I glance in his direction. We meet gazes for a brief moment. His brows knit together in concern as his gaze travels down the length of my body and back up. My nerves are frayed, so I'm not sure if I trust my own judgment, but I sense that he feels some modicum of sympathy toward me. Stripped down to my underwear, I feel naked before him. Embarrassed, I stare at the floor.

When he finally crosses the room, I keep my eyes averted until he walks out the door. Relieved to finally be alone, I sink onto the bed and cry. No sound utters from my lips. These are silent, fruitless tears. This situation is hopeless. I'm going to die here.

Moments later, Vance steps back into the room. I look up just as he wraps a large navy blue blanket around my shoulders. The wool scratches against my skin. Without saying a word, he turns and walks away, shutting the door behind him.

I huddle under the heavy weight of the blanket, drawing my feet curled up under me onto the bed. My vision won't fully focus, so I stare blindly at the wall as violent shivers slowly leave my body. Everything hurts. Mainly my jaw from chattering and clenching. I open my mouth widely and stretch the ligaments.

For the first time in the last twelve hours, I'm almost grateful. Given my situation, it seems impossible to feel gratitude, but I do. Grateful for something as simple as a wool blanket. An itchy, odorous wool blanket, but a blanket nonetheless.

My eyes close slowly, heavy as anchors. I'm so tired. As warmth returns to my limbs, I sink further into the bed. Ungracefully, I lie on my side, my hands still fixed behind my back. Drifting. I'm drifting away.

I hope I never wake up.

***

Eyes won't open. I hear them talking just outside my door, their voices grumbling quietly back and forth. I struggle to pull myself out of sleep and back to reality. My right arm is trapped under me and has fallen asleep. My right hand buzzes fiercely. My lethargic lids finally flutter open. Light streams through the window. I've slept maybe an hour by the looks of things. Desperate to give my shoulder relief, I roll to my stomach as slowly as possible, hoping to keep the bed from creaking. I don't want to draw attention to myself while listening to their conversation.

Vance keeps his voice low, just above a high whisper. "I don't get it. Why are we dragging it out? Last time, we had it done and over with within hours. I had her buried before dusk."

Jake doesn't bother to lower his voice. "Yeah, but that's the problem. It was too quick. Even the guy who bought it said so. Said we lacked creativity. I think if we offer more of a show, spice things up a bit, then we'll get a lot more money for it. Same guy hired us to do another, but said he wants better than last time. He handpicked this girl specifically. He's a sick bastard."

"Well, what does that make us?" Vance says.

"What, you suddenly have a conscience now, Vance? That girl in there? No one gives a fuck about her. You said it yourself. You've watched for a while now and she has, what, one friend? Who the fuck cares? Get over it."

His words slam into me. Who the fuck cares? He's right. Besides Terin, there's no one. Is anyone even aware that I'm gone? Terin's likely not even all that worried yet. She probably figures I snuck home last night and now I'm ignoring her texts. Again.

"Take that little scene with the hose," Jake says. "That's entertainment. That's what people want to see. They want a show."

"So what are you saying? We keep her around for a day? Two days? A week? How long are we talking here? People are going to start looking for her soon. Even if she doesn't have a lot of friends, they're going to eventually notice she's missing. Tomorrow is Monday and she'll miss work. She ain't the kind of girl who just skips out on work without calling in. I don't want police sniffing around before she's dead and buried. I'm not into that. I wanna get it done and leave the state. Like last time."

"I agree. We can't keep her around for long. I'm thinking we focus on the task at hand, give the camera a good few days of entertainment. Slap her around. Fuck with her a bit. Then finish the job before anyone even files a missing-person report."

Vance clears his throat. "So if he handpicked her like you said, does that mean he knows her?"

Jake lets out a disturbing laugh. "What do I care?"

Feels as if my heart is going to beat its way right out of my chest wall. It hammers away at an unforgiving pace. Listening to these men plot out my death, the last few hours, maybe days of my life, is surreal. My muscles shake with tension, ready to respond. I'm alert. Scan the room for answers. How can I get out of this? There is no way out of this bedroom other than the tiny window, which I doubt I can fit through. Or straight through the door, which is not an option with both men blocking the way. I doubt I'd get very far with my hands behind my back, anyway.

I need my hands free. This is essential. My mind races, seeking a way out of my restraints. I either need to break free of them, or I must convince them to untie me. This thought triggers another realization. I've barely spoken to them. I've been

63

too busy cowering and bawling my eyes out. What in the hell is wrong with me?

"Help. Please help."

Both men enter the room and stand beside the bed, gawking down at me, surprised that I've decided to speak.

"My arms are asleep. I can't feel them and I can't sit up. Please help." I writhe helplessly until the blanket falls away, exposing most of my body.

A gleam lights in Jake's eyes. "You want to sit up? Fine, then sit up." He reaches down and laces his thick fingers in my hair, yanking me into a sitting position. I yelp out as sharp agony sears through my crown, my hair straining at the roots. I'm so tired of this man pulling me around by my hair like a caveman. Blink back the tears. Focus.

On the edge of the bed, I tip my chin up and hope for mercy. "I have to pee too. Can you untie me?" I really do have to pee and I'm hoping this will be my chance. If not now, then I may not get a chance at all. Time is not my friend right now.

He bends at the waist and stares into my eyes. His breath hits my cheeks in hot waves. I'm surprised it doesn't smell. I see green flecks in his shit-brown eyes. "I don't give a damn if you have to pee. Piss yourself for all I care. Understood?"

I steal a peek at Vance. He's standing just behind Jake, staring at me intently. "Please?" I say to him.

Jake's flat palm strikes the side of my face and ear so hard that I fall to the right. My ear rings loudly. The vision in my left eye blurs. My face turns downward to the floor as I try to regain composure.

He tips my head back sharply so that I'm staring into his face at an awkward angle. His expression twists in ugly anger. "Did you not hear what I said? You're not getting out of these ropes, little girl. And don't you dare ask again. Got it?"

Nodding my head, I don't risk another glance in Vance's direction, but I know he's watching, deliberating. I don't know why, but he's not one hundred percent on board with this fiasco. I wonder how he got himself into it in the first place. He's not a nice guy, clearly. He has actively planned and executed my kidnapping, and plans to murder me. He has already killed Sheila Weaverton. Who knows how many others?

Still…something in him resists this outright violence and torture. I must feed into that.

"Stand up."

With shaky legs, I manage to stand upright. Jake doesn't step back, so we're practically chest to chest. I dare to look into his eyes again. I can practically see the gears in his mind running at full speed as he plans his next move. It's clear that he's flying by the seat of his pants, performing for the camera as he goes.

He looks to the camera, then back at me. He grabs me by the shoulder and spins me a quarter turn so I'm facing my witness, its red light winking at me. Now standing to my side, Jake reaches up and flips down one side of my bra until my nipple is exposed. He gives it a flick. Then pinches it. I bite my lip, refusing to cry out. In response, he slaps at my breast, bouncing it up and down like a basketball. It's more humiliating than painful, but I resist making any complaint.

He cracks a wicked smile. "I'm the boss here, you got it?" Now both hands fondle my breasts. When I don't answer immediately, he pinches both nipples simultaneously until I scream out and fall to my knees.

"Stand back up!" he barks.

Tears fall over my cheeks as I scramble back to my feet. I want to fight back. I need to fight back. I just don't know how. How can I possibly fight this man? This situation? Why is this happening to me?

When I'm on my feet he bends down until we're face to face, practically nose to nose. I avoid his evil eyes and stare at the pocked acne scars on his cheeks. I can no longer see Vance in my peripheral vision and I wonder if he's left the room or if he's simply watching the show.

"You have to piss, do ya?"

I'm not sure if I want to answer the question. I shake my head, "No, I don't have to go anymore."

"Sure you do. You've been here all day. Haven't peed since you got here. Hey, Vance!" His voice bellows through the cabin.

"Yeah?" Vance's voice travels from the other room.

"Bring that bucket in here. The one on the front porch."

"The bucket?"

Jake rolls his eyes. "Just do it!"

I tremble and wait for what's to come.

When Vance enters the room, Jake finally steps back. I turn to see Vance standing in the doorway with a blue five-gallon bucket dangling from his right hand.

"Bring it here."

I know where this is going. I take a small step back, shaking my head. "I said I don't have to go anymore. Please. I don't have to go."

Ignoring my plea, Jake snags the bucket from Vance and sits it directly in front of me. "There. Piss in that."

Wrists burn. Deep bruises ache. Joints scream out in agony. None of it compares to the all-consuming mortification that engulfs me. "Please. I'm fine. I don't have to go."

Jake's eyes narrow, flashing their warning. "Are you really going to fight me on this?"

I close my eyes and shake my head at him, knowing that I cannot win this fight. I must resign to the inevitable. When I open them, he stares at me triumphantly. Smug with his power.

My lip trembles as he lunges forward and jerks my underwear down with one swift motion. Avoiding the gaze of my audience—Jake, Vance, the ever-present camera—I stare at the wall opposite me.

"Now sit." He kicks the bucket so it's directly behind me.

My knees shake. My bladder spasms in anticipation. I really do need to pee so badly. Bending at the knees, and then at the waist so that I'm squatting perfectly over the opening, I focus on balance. The muscles in my thighs complain. I haven't eaten in over twenty-four hours and my body is weak. Despite having to go, my bladder holds on. I close my eyes and try to ignore the spectators. Hot, salty tears streak down my cheeks for the hundredth time since I've been here.

Finally, my pelvic floor muscles relax and my bladder releases. Relief floods my system.

"Now, turn and look at the camera while you go."

I stop mid-stream, my calves and thighs beginning to burn. Without looking at him, I take in a deep breath then turn and look at the camera. I stare into the glassy black lens, expressionless, dead inside, and finish my business.

CHAPTER SEVEN

Day two. I'm still alive but I'm beginning to wish for death. Everything hurts. Not a single cell of my body escapes the pain. Fortunately, the pain is only physical. Emotionally, I'm numb. Lifeless, spiritless. Maybe I'm already dead and I just don't know it yet. I'm stuck in limbo between living and dying, where the body still suffers and feels pain. It's a special kind of hell. I'm not going to survive this ordeal, so I can only wish for expedience at this point.

I slept fitfully throughout the night, half expecting Jake to wander in at any moment to create another spontaneous scene for the camera. It's clear that's his only goal. Creating worthy material for his project. He never did come back into the room that night. Once I finished peeing, Vance asked Jake if he should feed me and Jake told him to make me wait another day. "It'll break the last bit of fight in her," he said.

Seems to me that he'd want a little fight. It would add a little more drama. Then again, they don't plan to keep me around all that much longer.

As daylight returns, my thoughts stray. Dozing off and on, lids heavy, I lie on my mattress, huddled under the wool blanket. *I wonder if anyone has noticed I'm gone. The wood on the ceiling looks rotten. Surely Terin has realized something is wrong by now. I ignore her texts often, so maybe not. Mashed potatoes. Chicken. I'm so hungry. Will they kill me today?*

The door to my room slowly eases open. As if in a dream, I turn my head and look at Vance through droopy lids. Are there two of him? I feel drugged but I know it's just fatigue. A deep, deep exhaustion beyond anything I've ever known envelopes me.

The smell of food tempts my nostrils, teasing me into full consciousness. Eyes flutter. Focus.

"I brought you breakfast."

His tone is quiet and lacking emotion. It sounds deliberate.

It takes everything I have, but I roll to my side, and leverage myself to a sitting position. The rope around my wrists rubs against yesterday's scabs, tearing the crusty top layer away. It stings but I don't care. All I can think about is food. The blanket has fallen off my shoulders and covers my lap while I sit in my bra. I still don't care.

Vance crouches in front of me, a plate of steaming scrambled eggs and a light brown piece of toast in his hand. I lick my dry, chapped lips in anticipation. My mouth pools with saliva.

He looks at me, then at the plate, then back at me, contemplating how to move forward.

"You can untie me." My voice is foreign even to

my own ears. Scratchy and hoarse, like a lifelong smoker. "I swear I won't try anything." I couldn't if I wanted to.

I watch him ponder my offer, one eyebrow cocked. He shakes his head. "No, I don't think that's a wise decision. I'll feed you myself."

"Fine. Whatever."

Quietly, I let him shovel food into my mouth. I barely chew before swallowing, then opening for the next bite. He offers sips of water in between. Watching him, I gauge his mood. I still can't figure him out. Jake is easy. He's violent and unconscionable. A true sociopath. Vance. He's on the wrong side of the law but seems to do it out of necessity rather than desire. He's in the wrong profession.

"What in the hell is this?"

Vance startles and nearly drops the plate. With only half a plate of food gone, I'm still famished, but I glance in Jake's direction. He stands in the doorway, hands on hips. A flash of fear passes through me. Is today the day?

"I was just making sure she had a little food. You said she could eat today." Vance stands up and faces Jake.

"Well, that's nice and all, but we ain't making a children's video. We need something a little more raw, a little more gripping, if you know what I mean. Jesus, Vance, gimme that damn plate."

Vance hands over the plate and steps away. My eyes follow the plate. I know Jake is going to make me work for it but I don't care. Today is going to suck no matter what, and I'd prefer to have food in

71

my belly rather than not at this point.

"Look at me, woman!"

Understanding the routine, I do as he says and follow orders diligently. When our eyes meet, I try to squelch the rising fear. I'd prefer to maintain the welcoming sense of numbness that had embraced me when I woke up.

He bends at the waist and plops the plate on the floor in front of me, then straightens back to his full height and eyeballs me with a wicked sneer. "Now you may eat your breakfast."

My imagination scrolls through a variety of ways I can respond to this man. Most of them consist of screaming and clawing his eyes out. With hands secured behind my back, this option is not feasible. Nor would it end well for me.

I decide I will make this as boring of a scene as possible for him. I will comply obediently. With my chin up, I scoot to the edge of the bed, then awkwardly maneuver to my knees. Like a dog, I hunch over and lap up the scrambled eggs, hands secured behind me. With shame constricting my throat, I force the food down in tasteless lumps. I cough and choke on a bite, but swallow it down persistently. I am determined not to cause a scene this time. That's exactly what he wants.

Sensing his frustration, I take the last bite and sit back on my haunches, afraid to look at him directly. I stare at the camera instead and wait for his response.

I startle when he suddenly lets out a bellowing laugh. I look up at him, and though he's laughing, his face is beet red. I've angered him. Fear triggers

72

a cramping in my bowels and nausea rises. Too much food too fast.

His hand snakes out and his fingers twist around the hair at the base of my neck. Blinding pain travels from the base of my neck through the center of my skull and settles just behind my eyeballs. I clamber to my feet only to release some of the tension.

He wraps an arm around my shoulders and pulls me tight against him, as if we're old pals. "Tough girl, eh?" He leans down, pressing his cheek to mine so that we're both facing the camera as if posing for a photo. "All right then, tough girl. Let's play rough." He squeezes my shoulder tight, his thumbs digging into my flesh with a warning of what's to come. What have I done? Why have I spurred this man's anger further?

He spins me until I'm facing the bed. "Go on and get on your knees." When I don't respond quick enough, he spins me around so I'm facing him and punches me hard in the gut. My diaphragm spasms. I let out a whoosh sound as all oxygen is forced out of my lungs and I bend at the waist, gasping for air. The food I've just ingested threatens to come back up.

He doesn't allow me to recover before he spins me back toward the bed. "I said, get on your knees," he barks. "Leave the room, Vance. I want to be alone with her for a while."

Kneeling down, I look to Vance, still retching and desperate for air. He hesitates before he turns and walks out the door, shutting the door behind him. He's left. Fear overwhelms my senses. I'm alone with this monster. I have no doubt he'll rape me and God only knows what else, but I know it will involve pain. A great deal of it. I'm no longer numb or brave or determined to spite him. Tears find me again. I search the recesses of my brain for answers. Salvation. Anything.

"Lay your head down on the bed."

I do as I'm told and bend at the waist, placing my head on the mattress. I make sure to keep my head turned away from the camera. My knees dig into the hard wood floors.

Jake crouches down next to me, caressing one hand over my ass. I close my eyes in disgust. His hand draws back and then slaps my behind with one powerful swing. It stings down to the backs of my thighs. He spanks me over and over again until I lose count. With each slap, my body presses forward into the mattress, my ribs digging into the metal frame, knees scraping painfully against the wood in rhythm to my beating. I'm not sure when, but at some point I begin to whimper loudly between each assault. It's almost musical.

When he's done, he pauses for what feels like forever. His breathing is quicker, shallower, and I know he's aroused. With a quick jerk, he pulls me upright by my hair until I'm sitting on my haunches. My back is arched, and my neck juts out as I look to the ceiling.

"You like that?" he asks. "I bet you do. I bet you like it rough, don't you?"

No words come to mind. I'm fearful of responding to him. I don't know what he wants to hear.

74

He shoves my face back on the bed, but this time he makes sure I'm turned toward the camera. His hand strokes over my ass again. The flesh stings hot and swollen. Pressing my lips together, I brace for the next wave of spankings. Instead, his hand roams up my back, then back down my spine. He hooks a finger under the hip of my panties and pulls them to my knees. Vulnerable and exposed, I automatically bring my knees together, clenching my thighs as tight as possible.

He gives my ass one vicious slap. My muscles quiver in response. He laughs. "Slide those knees back out."

I shake my head.

"No? You're saying no?" Jake presses my head further into the mattress and shoves his hand between my thighs, tearing them apart. "There. Keep them like that. Don't move."

Resisting the urge to slide them right back into place, I close my eyes tight and wait. Why can't I fight back? How can I fight back?

Jake rubs my ass cheeks, first the right, then the left. When he slides a finger into me, it's more than I can bear. Revulsion fills my body. My stomach writhes like snakes low in my belly. I want to die. I'd rather die than experience this humiliation any longer.

His breathing is faster now. He presses his fingers further inside me. My full bladder spasms. Desperate to stop him from going any further, I cling to a sudden idea. Blocking out the sensations of his fingers, the fact that I'm on my knees being assaulted in front of a camera, I take slow deep breaths and concentrate on releasing my bladder. Suddenly, hot, wet urine streams down my legs.

"What the fuck?" Jake jerks his hand back and stands up.

I roll over and sit on the floor, my breath coming in quick, shallow bursts as I stare up at him. I'm shocked at my own bravado. I've outsmarted him and it fills me with both fear and elation.

I've peed all over him. It drips down his arm and has splattered all over his jeans and shoes. "You fucking bitch." His face contorts as rage consumes him. I hunker down and hunch my shoulders, knowing that I will pay the price for what I've done. But at least he's no longer inside me.

Anticipating the next move, I try to duck out of the way when he kicks out. His foot connects with my temple. I swoon and topple over. Stars cloud my vision. A barrage of kicks strike me up and down the length of my body. Ribs crack. I roll to the side. Spine. Hips. Back of the head. Nothing goes unscathed as he kicks me over and over again. Just let me die.

Vance swings the door open. "What in the hell, Jake?"

The kicking stops abruptly. "She fucking pissed all over me. Can you believe that?"

Everything hurts and throbs as I lay on my back, staring up at him through swollen eyes. Something drips down the back of my throat. I swallow. Tastes metallic. My mouth must be bleeding.

"She hasn't peed since yesterday," Vance answers matter-of-factly.

"Fuck you, Vance. I'm going to clean myself up.

76

Why don't you make yourself useful and clean the rest of this mess up. I'm done messing with this bitch. Let's just get it done with."

My vision is blurred and my ears ring so loudly I feel like I might go mad. Still, I know this is it. I no longer have any time. I roll to my side and watch Jake storm out of the room. Several parts of my body and face throb in unison to the fast pace of my racing heart.

Vance approaches and kneels in front of me, sizing up the damage. "Jesus, he made a mess of you, all right."

I dare to look him in the eye. He meets my gaze boldly. His jaw clenches. "Probably better this way. I'm tired of dragging this out. Best be done with it."

Hope leaves my body. He harbors no sympathy for me. He merely wants to be done with the whole ordeal so he can collect his money and move on. He's his own kind of crazy. He stands and places his hands on his hips. "I'll grab a towel to wipe up this mess."

When he walks out the door I start writhing and twisting in an attempt to wriggle my wrists free. The pain is unbearable, but so is the thought of dying here today, so I strain harder. Hope springs forward when one section of the rope inches over the fleshy part under the thumb. Inspired, I wrestle with more desperation. Sweat pools on my upper lip. I'm flailing about on the floor in my own urine, putting everything I have into getting free. The skin of my wrists shreds under the rope. My thumb is out. Now it inches quickly over the rest of my hand. My right hand is completely free. My heart gallops with hope. I scramble to my knees and work at the ties that still bind my left wrist to the bed. With a mix of desperation and fear, I'm shaking violently, making dexterity difficult.

I hear Vance return just as I loosen the last knot. "Shit."

I roll to my back, ready to fight. He slides to his knees and pins me down with his weight as he reaches for my free hand. Anticipating his move, I wait until he's directly above me, his head turned toward the task at hand. As he clambers to secure my wrist, I take my left hand, which is still bound with rope, wrap my wrist around the rope and grasp firmly. He's pressing against my diaphragm, making it difficult to take in a deep breath. Still, I'm determined. In one swift move, I lasso the rope around his neck. Surprised, he glances down and releases my free hand to remove the rope from his neck. With that hand now free, I reach up and grab the other end of the rope. Rage and hope surge through me. Using every muscle in my body, I pull.

Vance's eyes bulge and his face flashes crimson. His fingers dig at the rope biting into his flesh. Knowing this is it, that I won't get any other chances, I bear down and pull harder. Every muscle in my arms and stomach burns and screams for mercy. Spittle dribbles out of his mouth as he fights for air. He rolls to the side in an attempt to escape but I roll with him. Now I'm straddling him and looking into his face. It feels as if I'm holding my own breath while he fights for his.

I strain and strain, watching him lose the battle. I'm terrified that his strength will outlast mine. The whites of his eyes speckle with burst blood vessels. Finally, his lids flutter and the pupils roll back into his head just before they close. His body slowly goes limp. I hold for another minute, pulling even tighter just to be sure. My hands cramp and tremble.

He's dead. Releasing the rope, I scramble backward off his body, horrified, yet relieved. My arms shake uncontrollably from both adrenaline and muscle strain. I scan the room and push my hair away from my sweaty face. Jake will be back any minute. I assume he's outside cleaning up with the only running water, otherwise he would have heard the commotion.

With a sharp jerk, I yank the rope out from under Vance. My left wrist is still bound. I don't have time to untie it. My panties are still down around my knees, wet with urine. Unwilling to go completely naked, I opt to pull them up.

I run to the door and yank it open. The living area is empty. I dash toward the front door. Halfway across the kitchen, the door swings wide open. Jake stops abruptly as if confused. I swerve to the right, leaping toward the kitchen sink.

"What the fuck?" Jake says behind me.

I'm searching for something, anything that I can use as a weapon. A small frying pan lined with bacon grease still sits on the cook stove. A rusty sink holds a few dirty dishes. I want a knife.

I'm yanked back by my hair before I find anything of use. This time the force is enough to knock me to my ass. Pain shoots up my tailbone. Unfazed, I roll to my knees and crawl away, anxious to get away from him. My hair twists and pulls, but I strain against him in the opposite direction. He bends and grabs me by the waist, so I lean forward and sink my teeth into his calf. Even through the thick denim, I bite down hard enough that I draw blood. I feel the skin give and Jake screams. He releases my hair and gives me a thump on the side of my head. I lose my grip and fall back. I kick out with both legs, aiming for his knees. The force causes a loud crack to resound throughout the room. His face pales and he loses his balance, staggering to a crouched position. I've clearly managed a bit of damage but I know it won't last long. Jake is vengeful and I will pay dearly for this act. Remembering the way he kicked me before, I roll away as fast as I can. I reach for the leg of the kitchen table and pull myself up. As I stand, my gaze falls to the single plate and fork sitting before me. One limp piece of bacon lies in a dried pool of egg yolk.

Jake grabs me by the waist again. As he pulls me backward, my fingers wrap beautifully around the shaft of the fork. I twist from my torso and raise my hand in the air, bringing it down with as much force as I can muster, aiming for the only spot that will save my life. His eyes. The first stab misses and hits him in the cheek. He screams and releases me. Before he can pull away, I raise up again and then arc down hard, this time hitting my mark. The tines of the fork pierce through his eyeball and lodge deep enough that I cannot pull it out. Blood spurts into my face. Jake screams, both hands flailing for the fork.

I'm not done. I cannot leave him like this. He

will find a way to kill me. I turn back to the kitchen drawers. The first one has a few more eating utensils and some rat droppings. The second one down has what I'm looking for. I snatch the largest knife out of the drawer and turn to face my captor, who is still trying to dislodge the fork from his face. He's screaming, and when he finally pulls it out, a gush of blood streams from the wound. The eye automatically closes as he tosses the fork to the ground. He faces me with only one open eye. He's squinting it tightly, blinking repeatedly as it waters uncontrollably. The other bleeds profusely down his face.

"Agh! Fucking bitch!" he yells.

I lunge forward. He lifts his hands to protect himself but I'm at an advantage. I can see clearly. He strikes out at me but misses, his knee buckling under from pain as he takes a step. As his balance shifts, I take a wide swing and slice just under his collarbone. Blood seeps from the clean cut. I had been aiming for his throat. I jump back when he swings at me again. Even with his injuries, he's still stronger than me. If he gets the upper hand, I'm dead.

As he steps back, preparing for another lunge, I leap forward, and this time make sure my aim is straight. I feel the eerie sensation of the blade piercing through skin and nestling itself neatly into his flesh. It's deep. I cannot pull it out. Like Vance only minutes ago, Jake's eyes widen. Both fear and pain haunt his expression as his fingers flutter over the handle of the knife.

In shock, I step back and watch with fascination.

81

I know he's going to pull the knife out. That will be what finally kills him. With trembling knees, I stand by the kitchen table as he struggles with the knife, finally unsheathing it from his throat. He gurgles and coughs. Blood spurts from his mouth. He falls to his knees. Gaping up at me, his mouth opens and closes like a fish gasping for oxygen. A wasted effort.

Breathe in. Breathe out.

I watch him drown in his own blood.

CHAPTER EIGHT

Staring down at Jake's dead body, I go weak in the knees and kneel down to keep from passing out. On all fours, I'm in my urine-soaked underwear, swollen, black and blue from head to toe, blood on my hands and face, a rope still tied to one chafed wrist.

Jake stares back at me with wide, empty eyes. Everything I've been through over the last forty-eight hours rushes forward in a series of terrifying memories. Gasping for air, I'm hyperventilating. *Breathe in. Breathe out.* Hot, salty tears stream down my cheeks. I'm not embarrassed. I'm not humiliated. I'm no longer scared. Rage fills my insides and spills over each pore of my body. Every cell is consumed. I scream into the empty room. A sharp, piercing scream that tears through my parched throat and echoes my agony. It's not enough. I scream and scream until my throat is hoarse and unable to produce much more sound. Instead of easing this building tension, it feeds it until I'm a pressure cooker ready to blow.

I leap to my feet and cross the room to stand over his body. It's not enough that he is dead. I kick him over and over again, thriving on the pain that shoots up my foot as it connects with his limp body. I don't recognize the shrill sounds that escape my ravaged throat as my own. Have I lost my mind?

When that no longer feeds me, I march into the bedroom where Vance lies inanimate. His hands still clutch at his throat as if he's frozen in time. His face is purple and his eyes are open, glazed over with a glassy gleam.

I move past him and head for the camera, fixated on its ominous blinking red light. I snatch it from its cradle and throw it to the floor. Then I grab the tripod with both hands, yielding it like an ax. I raise it above my head before bringing it down with all of my rage and anger. Screaming my warrior song, unleashing all my fury, I bring the tripod down over and over again, breaking the camera into hundreds of pieces. Shattering its wretched history.

When I'm tired and need to catch my breath, I pause. I take in my surroundings, imagining how I must look. But there is no longer a witness to my plight. I'm still alone. More so than ever. And I have no idea where I'm at or how to get home, but I'm going to leave this place anyway. I can't get away fast enough.

I bend down and pick through the remnants of the camera. It takes some finagling, but I manage to extract the SD card. These memories are mine and mine only. I'll never allow this video out to the public. I will find a way to destroy it.

With it in hand, I snag the wool blanket from the

84

bed and wrap it around myself. I shuffle out to the living area in search of car keys. I don't see them right away, so I dig through Jake's front pockets and find them in the left side. I avoid looking at his face again. My hands are still covered in blood.

Without another look back, I leave the cabin. I march down the path and turn on the faucet. Daylight is quickly fading and I'm desperate to get out of here before darkness settles. The idea of being here at night initiates a flux of anxiety. Dropping the blanket to the grass, I run my hands under the cold water, then over my face, back under the water, and over my legs and arms. Scrubbing. Scrubbing, until my skin rubs raw, I continue to scour the filth from my body.

I'm shivering, so I turn off the water and toss the hose to the side. I pick up my blanket and focus on getting away from this place. Rounding the cabin again, I see the SUV off to the side, parked in tall grass, away from the dirt path. I click the remote keyless entry and the lights flash.

Once inside the vehicle, I don't waste any time turning it on and shifting it into gear. Tires spin as I press firmly on the gas. Hands grip the steering wheel. Knuckles are white. I turn on the heat.

I have no idea where I'm going. All I know is that I'm free.

CHAPTER NINE

Lights shine too bright. Sounds amplify and grate on every nerve. I lie quietly under the thin hospital blanket, worn thin and frazzled. I feel small, my skin translucent. Anger simmers gently underneath a thicker layer of fatigue. It took up residence inside me during my fit of rage against my captors and remains there still. Suppressed. But there. Bubbling.

The officer who has worked with me over the last many hours sits patiently at the side of my bed and waits for me to answer his last question. It's hard to focus over the noise in my mind.

I can't seem to stream together coherent sentences or even form full-bodied thoughts. I shake my head to clear the cobwebs. Earlier I refused pain meds because I fear letting my guard down. I desperately need to sleep, but I'm afraid to. The doctor insisted I at least take alprazolam to calm my nerves. It mixes with my weary blood and numbs me thoroughly. I sink further into the bed. Can I disappear?

"Miss Benson?"

I blink once and shake off wandering thoughts. "I'm sorry, Officer…?"

"MacGregor."

"Officer MacGregor. I've just…"

"You've had enough for one night."

With a thin smile, I nod. "Yes, thank you for understanding. I'm tired and probably a little drugged. And to be honest, I don't want to relive that nightmare anymore today, if that's all right with you." I'm shocked at how calm my voice is, given my desire to scream.

His smile is gracious, lending his boyishly handsome face a genuinely trustworthy quality. His calm demeanor gives me a much needed sense of security. "It's quite fine with me. You've been through a lot these past few days. I'm not sure when you slept last, but it's been nearly six hours just since you wandered into the precinct. Since then you've been examined by doctors, run through CAT scans, and questioned for hours about your ordeal. I'll let you get some rest. I have to warn you, though. In the morning I'm going to bring in photos so you can identify the men who assaulted you."

A shiver runs up my spine. "Photos?" I ask in alarm.

"Yes. After you wandered into the station, investigators searched for hours for the place you described. Your directions were a little confusing, but that's to be expected. I don't imagine you would have been paying attention to fine details when you made your way back into town. But they eventually pieced it together and found it."

Officer MacGregor pauses. I sense that he's carefully contemplating the best way to word the next few sentences. My patience grows lean. "Yeah, but why do I have to identify them. Isn't there enough identification on them? Driver's license? Wallet? Bank cards? Fingerprints, et cetera. Can't your team identify them with other means? I don't ever want to look at those men again."

With thumbs hooked in his belt, he rocks back and takes in a slow breath before answering. "Yeah, yeah, those are all means to confirm their actual identity. However, we still need you to confirm that yes, those are indeed the men who kidnapped you. It's all part of policy and procedure in cases such as this. Does that make sense?"

I close my eyes and take a shaky breath. "Yes. I guess that makes sense." Another thought weaves through the fog of my brain. "Wait. You said the police did make it out there…to the cabin?"

"Yes. That's right."

"And they're dead, right? Both of them?"

Realization and compassion passes over his features, softening them. He leans forward and places a hand over mine. I flinch. He waits and allows me to settle, keeping his warm palm securely over my hand. "They are both confirmed dead, Miss Benson. I promise you."

The breath I've been holding releases in one long sigh. "Okay, thank you. I…I guess I just needed to hear that. Call me Tessa, please."

Another long pause fills the room. The sound of my heart monitor echoes a steady rhythm, reminding me that I survived. I'm alive. I feel dead inside.

Officer MacGregor's gaze flits back and forth nervously and I know he has more questions for me. Though I'm tired and spent, I'm oddly comforted by his presence, so I wait patiently for what's to come.

When his hazel eyes settle back on mine, he speaks softly. "One of my officers sent over a few photos. From the scene, that is. He also gave me a thorough verbal report over the phone. Of course I'll go up there first thing tomorrow morning and get a look myself, but from what I can tell, it's pretty grisly up there. It's difficult to imagine someone such as yourself, young and thin, a librarian at that, being able to take on two strong, hostile men. I'm not sure how you did it, but it took a lot of bravery to do what you did."

I hold his gaze. "It wasn't bravery at all. I just did what had to be done. Otherwise I'd be dead by now."

His hand squeezes lightly. "That may be true, but you are brave. Most women would not have survived such an ordeal. Most would not have fought so fiercely and lived to tell the tale. I know it's hard to hear, but it's true."

Resistant to his choice of words, I remain silent.

"There's one other thing."

I sense what's coming. *Breathe in. Breathe out.* The heart monitor picks up the pace, reflecting my trepidation.

"The camera they found. It was smashed to pieces in the middle of the bedroom floor. You didn't mention it in your statement."

"Uh huh?"

"They've searched the cabin thoroughly and they can't locate the SD card. It's missing."

"Uh huh?"

"Having that card would be extremely beneficial to this case, Tessa. Do you know where it is?"

Without blinking, my tone is passive and flat. "I have no idea what you're talking about."

He leans back into the chair and lets out a deep sigh. "I see. Well, I'm guessing it was lost in the shuffle. I'm sure we'll find it eventually."

He's giving me a reprieve even though he knows I'm lying. I'm grateful for it, but panic sets in when I realize he plans to leave. When he stands, I reach for his hand. "Please don't go yet. I'm…I'm not ready to be alone." Sleep is closing in as the sedative seeps through my veins, but I can't stand the idea of being alone tonight. Nightmares will visit for sure, and I doubt my ability to cope with the torment of what they will bring.

"Is there someone you'd like me to call for you? Someone who could come stay with you? A friend? Family, perhaps?"

"Not yet. I'm not ready. Maybe in the morning. Can you stay for a while?"

He looks surprised but he doesn't refuse. He quietly sits back down and doesn't utter another word. The sounds of the hospital coalesce together as my eyes flutter. His tranquil presence blurs to only a shadow in the corner of the room. Everything fades to black.

CHAPTER TEN

I'm in a movie theater. The smell of heavily buttered popcorn permeates the air. Tom sits next to me, but his eyes are on the screen. Terror fills my body and I want to run out of the theater, but I don't know why I'm afraid. I squeeze Tom's hand and lean in, my lips close to his ear. "I want to go home."

He ignores me.

"Tom." I shake his shoulder and raise my voice. "Tom. I'm scared. I want to go home."

He still won't acknowledge me. Why won't he answer me? I look toward the screen to see what has engrossed him so completely. The movie is black and white. There's a girl tied to a bed in the center of a small room. The girl is me. I'm watching myself. I'm in underwear and a bra. I'm sobbing and begging for help. I look so broken, so weak, so pathetic.

Frantic, I scan the theater. It's full. Everyone is watching. They can all see. My body flushes and I break into a cold sweat. A deafening roar fills my ears. I open my mouth to scream but no sound comes.

"Tessa. Tessa. Wake up."

Tearing the covers from my body, I bolt upright in the bed. Reality of where I am, here and now, sift through the remnants of the dream. Hospital walls surround me in a low-lit room. The sound of monitors and an IV pump hum through the otherwise silent medical floor. Officer MacGregor looks down at me with a look of gentle concern. *Breathe in. Breathe out.*

"You were dreaming. You're okay. Everything is okay."

Glancing around the room one last time, I confirm that it's as he says. Nodding, I slowly sink back into the pillow. A faint tinge of light peeks through a slit in the curtain and tells me morning is near. I've slept for hours, though I don't feel rested at all. It feels as if I've been deprived of sleep for weeks. My insides feel hollow, like they've been spooned out. I'm empty. Devoid of any emotion.

He stands close to the bed, looking down with a look of concern. "Do you want to talk about it?"

I shake my head. "No. Did...did you stay all night?" His fresh stubble and sleepy eyes tell me he's had a long night in the recliner in the corner of the room.

He shrugs a shoulder. "Yeah, you asked me to."

I'm mortified. "I didn't think you'd actually stay. I thought maybe as soon as I fell asleep you'd leave. I'm sorry. I shouldn't have kept you. Your family must be upset that you've been gone all this time."

He shrugs again. "Eh, not really. The only one at home waiting for me is my dog. And she'll be all right. I had nothing better to do. Besides, I stepped out a few times to handle some things. Work, you know."

Still embarrassed to think he stayed while I slept, I avert my gaze. "Well, I'm still sorry that I kept you." I want to crawl under the covers and hide. I want to succumb to the heavy fatigue that plagues every muscle and sleep forever.

"It's fine. Really. I didn't mind. I do need to be going, though. But before I do, I need to tell you…a friend of yours called in a missing person report late last night."

I turn and meet his gaze. "Terin."

He nods. "Yeah, one of the guys down at the station called me up and said there was a woman who had put in a report. Said her best friend had gone missing after they were out late dancing the other night. Said she couldn't reach you by phone, but didn't worry too much until she went to your apartment and discovered you weren't there either. I guess she was pretty frantic, so I got her number and gave her a call. I know you said you didn't want to talk with anyone yet, but I'm afraid she wouldn't hear of it."

I should be eager to see her but I'm not. I don't want the questions. I don't want to give answers. I just want to hide. "She's here, isn't she?"

His brows pinch together. "Yeah, I'm sorry. I've done my best to keep her at bay while you slept. She promised to stay in the waiting room until I gave her the go-ahead, but she's not going to leave

93

until she sees you herself. She's very stubborn."

I let out a sigh. "Yes. Yes, she is. It's fine. I appreciate your help. Really. You've been amazing. Go ahead and let her in. I'll be okay."

"You sure?"

No. I'm not. "Yeah, I'm sure."

He cocks his head to the side, as if contemplating whether he believes me. "All right then. I'll be back later today, though."

I suddenly remember our conversation of the previous evening. He'd said I'd have to look over photos and ID the men who kidnapped me. The men I killed. A lump rises in my throat and I find it hard to speak. I bite my lip to keep it from trembling and simply nod.

When he leaves the room, I take one deep breath after another, preparing for the onslaught of energy that will soon walk through that door. She'll want more than I can possibly give her right now. I have nothing to offer.

Expecting a storm to bust into the room, it takes a moment to process the sound of a gentle knocking at the door. It takes all my energy to pull myself to a sitting position. Sore muscles complain and a deep ache stems from the depth of my bones.

Terin peeks her head inside the door. Her face is free of makeup. Tear-streaked. When her red-rimmed eyes meet mine, both concern and relief wash over her features. She pushes the door wide and rushes forward.

She stops short at the foot of the bed, wringing her hands as if unsure of how to proceed. I can only imagine how I look, black and blue and swollen.

94

Broken. Damaged.

I know what she needs, so I hold out both arms and welcome her in.

Tears burst over and spill down her cheeks as she rounds the bed and sits next to me. Her thin arms wrap around my shoulders and pull me in. I want to feel something. I want to shed a tear, or scream out in anger, or feel a smidge of happiness to see that my dear friend has come to see me. I should feel relief and gratitude that I escaped. I should be rejoicing that I'm alive.

Numb, I rub her back and listen to her cry for the both of us.

CHAPTER ELEVEN

Officer MacGregor sits at my bedside, his hands folded neatly in his lap. An empty manila envelope lies next to me as I slowly flip through one photo at a time. I sense both he and Terin holding their breath. I take my time, my movements deliberate. I feel a strange detachment as I peruse the evidence of my captivation and unleashed violence.

Yes, anger, shame, hatred, fear, terror, and a multitude of ambiguous feelings that I cannot quite name flow deep within me, an undercurrent of muddled emotion. I feel they will never really leave. They are embedded at my core. Part of me now. Yet, as I inspect the evidence before me, I cannot fully connect with it. I thought seeing photos of the men, their bodies, the cabin, would send me into a tailspin of fear and terror. Instead, I'm agitated. My skin tingles. I want to scratch at my arms and legs. I feel the weight of Terin's and Officer MacGregor's stares. I can hear their thoughts. They're waiting for my reaction.

Why can't they leave me alone? All of them.

A photo of the front of the cabin taken from the driveway. *Flip*. The camera, smashed to bits. *Flip*. A plate with bacon and spatters of blood. *Flip*. The bed. *Flip*. Jake. Staring up at me, mocking me even from death. An ugly gash in his throat. A bloodied eyeball. Blood pooled around his head. *Flip*. Vance. Face mottled purple and blue from strangulation. Poised in death as if still fighting for life. Agitation bubbles inside of me. I hate them. They have escaped the terror. I have not. I still live with it. It is inside of me. Forever.

I want to scream and tear the photos into a million pieces. I breathe in and out, maintaining my composure in front of my small audience. I want to be done with this. I hold up one of the many photos of Jake. "This one was named Jake. I killed him with a knife after I stabbed him in the eye with a fork."

My tone is flat. I pull out the next photo. "This guy was Vance. He's the one I first saw in the library, the week before, and then again in the bar that night. He's the one who followed me. He found me in the alley after I left the bar. I strangled him to death with the rope they had tied me to the bed with. But I've gone over all that with you before. You know the details. And now I've confirmed it." I toss the photos to the edge of the bed while holding Officer MacGregor's gaze. "Are we done?"

I feel Terin staring at me in shock but I cannot look at her. I sense she's silently afraid of what I've been through, what I've survived, but mostly, of what I've done to those men.

He gathers the photos. "Yes, we're done with

photos. I'm sorry, Tessa, but it had to be done. Policy and procedure."

"Sure. Whatever."

He slips the stack of photos into the envelope. "They still can't find the SD card for the camera."

My patience thins. "Yeah?"

"At some point, someone removed it." His voice is calm, laced with firm determination.

"Yeah?"

"Tessa, if you have that card, I would appreciate it if you handed over. It's evidence."

The infinitesimal thread that has been keeping me together pulls so tight it hums and then finally snaps. My tone is low and direct. "Listen, I'm going to tell you this once and once only. I lied before. I did take the SD card, and there is no way in hell I'll ever hand it over. It's mine. I told you everything you need to know about what happened between me and those bastards. You have photographic evidence. You don't need video. Now leave me the hell alone!"

He holds up his hands. "Calm down, calm down. I didn't mean to upset you. And to be fair, I didn't even want to ask you about it again. I completely understand where you're coming from. The Chief, my boss, pressed me about it today, and I felt obligated to ask. I promise I won't ever bring it up again. As far as I'm concerned, it's gone. Okay?"

His tone is genuine, but I can't shake this growing restlessness.

A nurse bustles into the room, a clipboard tucked under her arm, and interrupts the building tension. "Sorry to interrupt, but I have good news. I'm processing your discharge papers!"

Her smile lights up the room and I want to hide away in my dark shell. I clasp the sheets in my sweaty palms. "Discharge papers?"

"Yep. Doctor says you can go home first thing tomorrow morning. He'll make his rounds, then write orders. After he's done, I'll process the final forms and then you'll be good to go first thing. Sound good?"

I don't know what I want. This place is getting to me. The sounds. The smells. The lack of privacy. A nurse poking at me every hour. The idea of leaving the safety of these four walls sounds just as awful. How do I go home after this? How and when do I go back to work? How do I go back to the real world and pretend that I'm all right? I'm not fucking all right.

I nod and reach for the clipboard. "Sounds good."

"So, will you be going home or will you be staying with family for a while?"

"You're coming home with me," Terin says before I can respond.

Holding the pen in mid-air, I stare up at her with relief. She somehow knows exactly what I'm thinking.

"At least for the first night. We'll stay up late and talk, or you can go to bed early. Whatever you want. After a day or two we'll figure out when and if you want to go home. Okay?"

"Okay." I sign the forms, then stare out the window as the nurse mindlessly reads through a series of preliminary instructions for care. A flux of thoughts and feelings ebb and flow throughout my body. I can't decide which emotion I'm experiencing from one moment to the next. I'm afraid. I'm angry. I'm ambivalent. I'm numb. I'm agitated. I'm thin air.

I'm about to leave the hospital and return to society. Then what?

***

Morning comes after a restless night. I don't have to look into a mirror to know dark bags reside under my eyes. I feel the puffiness with every blink against dry, scratchy eyes. Restless agitation fills my body. My stomach growls.

Terin strolls through the door with two to-go latte cups, one in each hand, and a tentative smile on her lips. She has a brown paper sack tucked under her arm. "Coffee, my friend. And pumpkin bread. Your favorite."

I offer a forced smile. "Thanks."

Her grin wanes as she sets both coffees down and sits on the foot of my bed. "Hey, I know you're not feeling all that great and it's completely understandable, but the nurses tell me you aren't eating."

Avoiding her direct gaze, I look toward the coffees. "I've had a few bites here and there. I'm just not all that hungry yet."

"Yeah, well, as your best friend, I don't give a crap. You need to eat. From what I've been told, it's likely been since I saw you last Friday, before you went missing, that you ate much of anything. So, just humor me and eat a few bites of this pumpkin bread. Okay?" She holds the bread out directly in front of her, elbow locked with determination.

I don't want to fucking eat. Without saying a word, I hold out my hand and wait for her to pass the bag over. My mouth waters as I peel open the bag. My body clearly needs the nutrition. I'm not sure why the idea of food repulses me.

I nibble at the soft bread. It's moist and rich in flavor. It crumbles perfectly with each subsequent bite. It's simultaneously delicious and disgusting. I fight the urge to gag. Terin and I sit in silence. After a quarter of it is gone, I slip the remainder inside the bag.

Terin purses her lips with disapproval. "Well, it's not much, but it's better than nothing, I guess."

I nod. A scream tickles the back of my throat, itching to let loose into the sterile hospital room.

"Today is the day. I'm bailing you out of this joint! Isn't that great?"

Hopeful desperation. She so badly wants me to talk to her. Respond in any way, but it's too much effort. I just want to close my eyes and drift away. A long pause fills the room. Her eyes flit about nervously, attempting to focus on something, before finally landing on the coffee. She picks one up and sips carefully. Her tone is timid when she speaks again.

"Tess?"

"Yes?"

"That night at the club. Why did you leave? I looked for you for a while, and at first I thought maybe you snuck off with Tom somewhere, but

101

then I saw him again later, dancing with a few different women, so I assumed you left. But you don't usually leave me like that. I called but you didn't answer your phone. I should have come looking for you...I'm sorry..."

That night, the music, and alcohol, flood back. I close my eyes and lay back on the pillow. *Please stop asking me questions.* "Don't do that to yourself. It's not your fault. I was with Tom. For a bit. We argued. So I headed home."

"You and Tom argued?"

I can't do this right now. Opening my eyes, I stare up at the ceiling. "Can you do me a favor?"

She perks up. "Of course. What do you need?"

I raise my head off the pillow so I can look at her straight on. "Can you go to my apartment and grab some clothes? If I'm going to get out of this place, I'll need something to wear. I'll call ahead and get the manager to open the door for you."

"Yeah, yeah, sure. No problem."

"Now?"

Her facial muscles relax, transforming her anxious smile into recognition and hurt. She knows I'm trying to get rid of her. I don't care. I need space.

"Umm, sure." She stands and stares down at me awkwardly before finally turning away. She pauses in the doorway and turns. "I have a few other things to do while I'm out, but it shouldn't take me too long. I'll be back in a few hours. That work?"

Yes, fine. Just leave. "Sounds good."

The door closes quietly behind her and I sink into the bed with relief. I just want to be left alone.

102

Is that too much to ask? Everyone has questions but I don't have answers. I close my eyes and concentrate on letting the tension out of my body. The sound of the door opening jerks me right back. Muscles rigid, my eyes open and focus on the person entering my room.

I blink, wondering if I've drifted off to sleep and I'm dreaming.

"Tom? What are you doing here?"

He steps into the room and quietly pulls the door closed behind him before facing me with a gentle, almost nervous smile. "I heard what happened on the news and I had to come see you for myself. I had to know if you were okay."

My heart skips a beat and a thin layer of sweat breaks out over my already sensitive skin. I want to hide under the covers. "I...umm...I'm surprised to see you here after the..."

He holds a hand up and steps forward. "I know, I know. I'm sorry about that. I really am. I don't know what came over me. I had too much to drink, I guess. That's one of the reasons I came. To apologize. It's just that you looked so good. I got carried away."

Doubt writhes like snakes in my belly, warning me of lies and betrayal. I remember the way he tastes in my mouth, warm and salty. His assault was only the beginning of my nightmare that evening. Somehow, I feel he is to blame, though that is ridiculous. It was my fault for falling all over him like a lovesick schoolgirl. Nausea wells up and threatens to bring up the pumpkin bread.

He pauses, his brows pinched together as if he's

contemplating his next move. "Speaking of the other night…what did you tell the police?"

My brows furrow, reflecting my mirrored confusion. "Tell the police about what?"

"About me. And you. That night. Do they know we were together that night?"

I pull myself up in bed so I'm able to look into his face better. "I haven't said anything about you at all, Tom. It's not exactly something I want people to know."

His shoulders relax. "Okay, good. I was afraid they'd want to talk to me and ask me a bunch of questions."

"Even if they did, what would it matter?"

He shrugs and looks toward the ground sheepishly, a gesture that seems forced. "Oh, well, it wouldn't. I guess. I just don't know what to expect. I wasn't sure what you'd tell them about me, or us. This whole thing is just unbelievable. Frightening."

"Don't worry about your reputation, Tom. I'm sure it's still intact."

"That's not what I'm saying, Tessa," he says defensively, his eyes meeting mine once again. "I just wanted to know what you told them so I was prepared for them if they wanted to talk to me. That's all. I really am sorry about what you went through."

A million different responses run through my mind simultaneously. I sit silent and wish I could say even just one of them, but they all fight for attention.

"Do they know why those men did what they did? Do they have any leads on whether or not anyone else might have been involved in your kidnapping?"

I run my tongue along my teeth and wish I had a toothbrush. My mouth tastes terrible and feels like I'm growing hair on the inside of my mouth. "Why all the questions, Tom? What does it matter to you? You and I are done. Remember?"

He shrugs. "I'm just worried about you. I want to know that you're safe."

"Where is my phone?"

His lashes flutter. He's processing. "Your phone?"

"Yes, I had it with me that night and I think I left it in your car, with my handbag. I want it back."

He shakes his head, lips pursed together tight. "Nope. I haven't seen your phone. You must have lost it before then. I don't have it."

I know he's lying. I don't know how or why he would lie about it, but I know he is. "Hmm, okay. Well, like I said, I didn't say anything about you at all, so thanks for coming by. Your reputation will go unmarred. You can leave now. I'm tired."

He hesitates. "I can only imagine. I'll let you get some rest. Let me know if you need anything, though. I'd like to help, if I can."

I hold my breath and clench my jaw as he reaches out and lightly caresses my jawline with one finger. "Sweet Tessa. Whatever will I do with you?" The faraway quality of his tone gives the impression that he's talking to himself more than me. It sends goosebumps over my flesh. He bends over the bed and places a light kiss on my forehead. Heat rises up my neck and blushes my cheeks.

I watch him turn and leave. I want to scream and throw something at the back of his head. Another piece of me wants to ask him to stay. I can't help but think he's purposely messing with my head. Maybe I'm paranoid. Maybe, just maybe, he has feelings for me. A flutter of hope rises. Shame immediately shoves it aside.

Even now, I'm still a stupid girl.

***

A knock wakes me. Disoriented, I bolt upright in my bed. I'm in the hospital. I'm alive. *Breathe in. Breathe out.*

An unfamiliar face peeks through the cracked door. "Miss Benson?"

"Who are you?" Why can't people just leave me alone?

She steps into the room and closes the door behind her. All business, her hair is pulled back into an unforgiving bun. A form-fitting beige pantsuit matches perfectly with a light tan briefcase. Despite a bird-like lanky frame, she exudes bold confidence. I want her to leave.

"My name is Linda Wilkes. I'm with *The Seattle Times*. I'd like to talk with you for a bit. Ask you a few questions about the ordeal you went through."

My heart rate picks up. I scoot up into a sitting position, holding the blanket to my chest defensively. "What? No. I don't want to talk about it with you or anyone else. Who let you in here? Please leave."

She unzips the front zipper of her briefcase and

pulls out a recorder. With a sharp click, she turns it on. "Can you describe the events that led up to the moment you were captured?"

Pulling the thin blanket up higher, my voice tightens as I speak. "I told you. I...I don't...I can't talk about what happened. I don't want it in the papers."

"But it's already been in the papers, Miss Benson. You're a hero. A local phenomenon. You beat incredible odds and survived a horrific experience. Don't you want to tell your story to the world?"

My skin is covered in cold sweat and my heart races so fast I fear I might go into cardiac arrest as this strange, rude woman invades my privacy. I picture my face spattered all over the news. People gossiping about what those men did to me. It's a struggle to talk between short, shallow breaths. "No. I don't want to share my story with anyone. Please..."

"How did you manage to get away? I mean, it must have taken exceptional composure and bravery to take on your captors, knowing that at any moment they could kill you. How did you get the upper hand in such a harrowing circumstance?"

I feel the heat rise to my face and neck as embarrassment and frustration consume me. My voice rises another octave. "Why aren't you listening to me? I said I don't want to talk to you. Now leave."

She holds a hand up. "Okay, okay, settle down. No need to yell."

I slap the bed. "Yes, yes, there is a reason to yell.

You're not listening to me. Why doesn't anyone ever listen to me?" I toss the blanket to the side and climb out of bed. The room spins as soon as my feet hit the cold linoleum and I stand to my full height. I haven't eaten more than a few bites today and I haven't stood up except to use the restroom. I glance toward the mirror on the wall and don't recognize the disheveled, wild-eyed reflection staring back at me. Bluish bruising fades to a sick yellow hue speckling a good portion of my skin from head to toe. My hair is a tangled mess. The hospital gown hangs loose on my skeletal frame. I'm a member of the walking dead.

Looking away, I shake my head and fight through the fog, I take a step forward, pointing a finger in her face. "Like you. I told you to leave. You won't. I told you I don't want to answer your questions. You don't give a shit. No one ever listens."

The room spins faster. I lean on the side of the bed, my right hand bracing me as I gasp for air. I know I'm hyperventilating but I can't stop it. This woman needs to leave. "Stand up for yourself, they say. Speak up and state your mind, they say. But when I do, no one will ever fucking listen, so what's the point?"

The door bursts open and Officer MacGregor steps inside, one hand poised above his gun holster. His eyes dart back and forth between me and the reporter. "You need to leave."

The reporter appears stunned by the sudden appearance of a police officer. She puts her hands up. "No harm done, sir. I was simply asking Miss

Benson a few harmless questions."

Another wave of dizziness overwhelms me. I turn and brace both hands on the side of the bed for support, my knees weak and shaking violently. I stare down at the white bedding, hoping to focus and regain stability. "Leave. Everyone. Just. Leave." My demand is barely a breathless whisper. I feel robbed of my own rage.

Officer MacGregor pushes past the reporter and rushes to my side. He guides me to the bed. "Sit down. I'll call the nurse."

I brush his hands away, ashamed of my perpetual displays of weakness. I'm tired of living with myself. "I'm fine. Really." I turn and plop onto the bed before I pass out. "Just go...please..."

Even now, as I'm begging to be left alone, no one listens. They stare at me dumbly, disbelief on their faces. Like I'm too stupid to know what I really want or need. My fingers dig into the mattress by my sides. "GO! Just go!" I scream, using every last bit of strength. "Please, just go!" I continue to scream over and over again until there is no longer oxygen in my lungs. Blood rushes to my face.

A flurry of activity fills the room while I scream. The reporter scurries out of the room. Officer MacGregor darts to the doorway and hollers something down the hall. Three nurses, one female, two male, barge in. They surround me. Still screaming like a crazed banshee, I kick out and land a solid blow to a shin. An arm wraps around my shoulders. I buck back and my skull connects with bone or cartilage, I'm not sure. Someone barks out orders. *Secure her arms...the IV is in the*

109

left...Ativan now.

Even now, as I fight and scream in hysterics, a piece of me separates from the moment. Disengages and watches from a distance. Again, my power, what little I have of it, is stolen. I know I'm out of control. I'm irrational. The part of me that acts out cannot rein it in. The brewing storm has been unleashed. It will not relinquish until it has expelled all of its glorious rage. I scream even as the sedative washes over me, flooding my system with a false sense of euphoria. I'm heavy with it. I scream but only a muffled garble passes over my lips. *Don't quiet my storm. Don't quiet m...*

CHAPTER TWELVE

I'm strapped down. Rage wells up and sears every cell in my body. I want to scream and fight but rational thought has returned. Hysterics is what put me here in the first place. I broke the rules. I fought against those who refuse to listen. *Breathe.* I need to be smarter this time. I need to play nice and follow the rules. I just want out of here.

Staring up at the white ceiling, I know I'm in another ward of the hospital. The psychiatric ward, no doubt. I wait for shame and guilt to wash over me. They don't. Searching for their ever-lingering presence, I reach into every nook and cranny of my mind. Nothing. They're absent.

Curious, I do a mental check-in and evaluate my emotional state. I'm clearheaded. Not scared. Not ashamed. I'm not even flat or tired as I was before. I feel…I just want to get the hell out of this place. I know I must bide my time and wait. I close my eyes and go inward. This could take some time.

Three days pass while doctors monitor my every move. They speak in soft, non-aggressive tones, while asking the same set of programmed questions in multiple forms, hoping to gauge my emotional state, trying to elicit a response that may indicate whether I'm still "unstable" or not. I refuse to talk more than necessary, so they talk for me or about me as if I'm not even there. That's fine. Whatever makes them feel better.

When I do speak, it's calm and diligent. Quelling the roiling storm within. It lingers there. Inside. Bouncing off each nerve ending, spurring me on. But I remain quiet and play by their rules.

When the doctor finally signs my release papers, I sit placidly in the wheelchair and wait for Terin to wheel me out to her car. I want to run.

Fresh, cold air smacks me in the face as we pass through the sliding doors. My cheeks and lips sting. Frost covers the grass. The smell of the city permeates the air but I welcome it. Anything is better than the scent of the hospital.

The sounds hit me differently. Sirens echo in the far-off distance. Tires against pavement, honking, engines revving, a crying baby in the parking lot. Anxiety wells up but I keep my head down and try to shut it out.

Once we're in the car, Terin buckles up, starts the ignition and we pull onto the road. Air blasts from the heating vents. Alternative rock music plays on the radio, fraying my nerves. I reach over and turn it off.

Terin flashes a nervous grin but says nothing. I know she's confused. I'm her best friend but she no longer knows what to say to me or how to interact with this dull, hollow shell that I've become.

112

"Take me home, Terin."

"That's the plan. I've got the spare bedroom ready for you. It's tiny but it should do."

"My home, Terin."

She shoots me another nervous glance. "What are you talking about? We agreed you'd stay with me."

"I know, but that was before. Now I just want to go home."

Her eyes are on the road as she navigates a left turn. "But the doctor said it would be best if you had friends or family around for a while."

"Terin. Look at me."

She waits until we are at a complete stop at the next red light, then turns to me with a look of trepidation. Her brows are furrowed with worry.

"I want to go home. I need some time alone."

"But…"

Squelched tension builds in my voice. "No buts. I'm fine. I know I had a freakout and it scared everyone. But I promise you, the best thing for me right now is a little space. I'm overwhelmed. Please, just for once, I need someone to listen to what I'm saying and respect it. I. want. To. Go. Home."

Her tongue darts out and she licks her dry lips. "Okay, I don't like it, but if that's what you need, then I'm supportive. But you have to promise to call if you need anything at all. Do you understand me?"

I nod. "Yes."

"I'm serious. I really don't like this, and in order to respect your request, this is what I've got to have in return. I need to know you'll reach out if you need me."

"I will. I promise."

As she parks the car, I take in my neighborhood. I've been away one week, but it feels like a lifetime. It looks different somehow, changed. Or maybe I'm the one who changed. How could I not?

Terin flits about, opening the car door, hovering at my side, carrying my small case of toiletries that she'd brought. Her speech is hurried and sporadic. "When I was here earlier, to get your things, I made sure to turn up the heat. I watered your plants, so there's no need to worry about that…"

My mind wanders as I focus on taking one step after the other toward my apartment. It all seems so new. My senses feel heightened, awakened, as if I'm able to feel my surroundings better than I ever have. I'm a raw nerve. Why is that? It fascinates me. The sidewalk has varied cracks and breaks from years' worth of winter freezes. Dead, brown leaves scatter over the ground. The bricks on the building have faded in color with age. On the far corner, a dead rose bush garnishes the bleak landscape. Has that always been there? How have I not seen these details before?

Someone crossing the street catches my eye. He turns just as I face him and walks away with a hurried step. His gait and build are familiar. Tom? But he's wearing jeans and a black hoodie. Not something Tom would wear. I shake that idea away and watch him round the corner, ashamed that part of me wishes it was him.

"Wait, what about food?" Terin hovers on the sidewalk, expectation animating her features. "You're going to need to restock your fridge. I doubt anything's any good by now. I'll have to run to the store and do some shopping for you."

I reach out and touch her shoulder. "I'll be fine. I'm going to lay low for today but tomorrow, I promise I'll make my way to the store." I suddenly remember that I no longer have my driver's license. It was in my handbag that night, with my phone. I'll need to go to the DMV soon. That thought nauseates me. Thank goodness I didn't take my debit card that evening. Just cash.

"Are you sure? I can run down the road right now and pick up a few items. It's no big deal."

"Stop worrying over me. I'm not going to starve to death. Okay?"

She bites her lip. "Okay. There's a few snacks in the little bag I packed for you. Eat that."

We're both quiet as we make our way inside the entrance, down the hall, and to my unit. Terin pulls out my key and fumbles with it until it finally engages. I step into my home. A vast emptiness fills the cool air. It's not familiar. It looks organized and tidy and lifeless. Beige carpet. Beige curtains. Matching tan couch and loveseat. A beige afghan drapes over the back of the couch. Where is the color? The character? This is where I live. It's bland and boring. It's uptight and lonely. Everything that represents who I am. Correction. Who I was. This realization piques my interest. Goosebumps raise over the surface of my skin.

The girl who lived here before is gone. Not just gone, but dead. I dig deep and search for any emotion related to this realization. Nothing. I will not miss that girl. Good riddance.

What does frighten me is that I have no idea who replaced her.

CHAPTER THIRTEEN

I stare up at the ceiling fan and remember when I had thought it looked like a starfish in the dark. Now it only looks like a ceiling fan. I rub my feet together under the blankets in an effort to warm them. My toes have felt like ice packs all day. I roll to my side, facing the bedroom window. A starlit sky blinks at me. Rare for this time of year, when it's typically overcast and drizzling. I bet it's nearing freezing temperatures out there. I wonder how many homeless are suffering. The word *suffering* brings a barrage of memories to the surface. Flashes of my kidnapping. Images of the cabin. Peeing into a bucket. A camera staring at me. Jake's foot kicking me over and over again. Pain. Shame. Fear in my bones.

A cold sweat breaks out over my skin. Rage bubbles up to the surface and boils my insides. I want to squeeze or punch something. I grip the sheet in my hands, fighting to chase away the memories. I replay those last moments in the cabin. How I unleashed my fear and fury on my kidnappers. I think of how it felt to watch them die. How it felt to fight back. The way it filled the hollowness that has always haunted me. How it squelched the torment of what I'd been through. It wasn't enough. I have more inside of me that aches to come out. My heart hammers in my chest, echoing that need.

The digital red numbers of my alarm clock seem brighter than usual against the darkness of my lonely room. It's one forty-seven a.m. I squeeze my eyes tight. I still see red behind my lids, or at least I think I do. It reminds me of the blinking red camera light and I want to throw it across the room. I roll over, kicking my legs in an effort to keep the blankets from tangling around my legs. I lie there for a good while before I realize I'm staring at the wall. Have I even blinked? I roll to my back and stare at the ceiling again. I'll never fall asleep like this. I need to get up and find something else to think about.

I toss the blanket aside, giving up on the idea of sleep for the third night in a row since I've been home. Slipping into an oversized sweatshirt, it swallows my thinning frame. My appetite has yet to return. I pull on warm fuzzy socks and leave my bedroom without a plan.

I find myself in the bathroom down the hall, staring at my reflection in the mirror above the pedestal sink. How did I end up in here? I don't even remember turning on the light. Leaning forward, I peer at the skin under my eyes. A purplish hue reveals my lack of sleep. Healing bruises reflect an ugly yellowish-green tint. I pucker my lips and inspect the sunken look of my cheeks. I've never thought of myself as pretty or not pretty. Just average. Now, what I see staring back makes the hair on my arms prickle. This woman disgusts me. I want to scream and imagine my fist smashing through the center of the mirror, through the center of her face. That's crazy. Instead, I step back, take a deep breath, then flip her off before turning away. With a flick of the light switch, I walk out of the bathroom.

Agitated, I wander the apartment, picking up every knick-knack and examining it thoroughly for its purpose. I don't have a lot of useless things, but even the ones I do strike me as so trivial. I hold up a thin vase that sits on an inset bookshelf in the living room. It's empty. Why? It's meant to hold flowers. Yet, here it sits, pointless and meaningless in my care. I imagine throwing it across the room and watching it shatter into a thousand pieces. Such a satisfying image. I set it down slowly and walk away.

That's exactly how I feel. Pointless and meaningless. I've holed up in this apartment for three days and I'm restless. I could go somewhere. I *should* go somewhere. A little fresh air would be good for me. A rush of excitement zings through my body as I dart to the bedroom and snag a pair of baggy sweats from my dresser.

Back to the living room, I open the closet in search of a warm jacket. As I slip into a puffy coat, I remember it's the middle of the night. Paused, both hands frozen in place on the zipper, I'm distraught and confused. I can't go out at these hours. I want to, though. Why can't I? I just need some fresh air.

The old Tessa wouldn't dare go out at this hour. She'd be too terrified. But that girl is gone. Am I scared now? I search inward, expecting fear and trepidation. I'm not afraid. Not yet. I need to get out of this damn apartment. I zip up the coat, grab my keys off the counter, and head out the front door before I can analyze it any further.

Once outside, the frigid night air hits my face and invigorates my whole being. I stand on the sidewalk and look right, then left. The streets are empty. Frost covers every windshield. My heart races and I rub my hands together in nervous anticipation. I have no idea where I'm going, but it feels good to be out of that stuffy building. I take a left.

Three blocks down, I sense the space between myself and the apartment expanding beyond my comfort level. My pace slows as my bravery wavers. I don't know if I can do this. I zip the zipper up the last inch so that it's nestled just under my chin. Another block or two, then I'll head back.

With my head down against the wind, I squelch my internal dialogue and put one foot in front of the other. There's nothing to be afraid of. The sound of a man's laughter gains my attention and my chin snaps up. Almost to the corner of Jefferson and Third, I scan the area and don't see anyone. I round the corner and look down the street. A small group of men stumble out of the pub half a block down. By the sound of their ruckus I know they're drunk out of their minds. I scoot back behind the brick of the building. My breath plumes in front of my face in short bursts. I need to get home.

I turn and hurry back the way I came. Their voices echo somewhere behind me. I can't tell if they are following me or not. I can't bring myself to look back, but now I'm panicked. It's hard to breathe. My chest tightens. I break into a sprint. All I can hear is my brisk breathing echoing in my ears and my feet slapping against the pavement. Empty stores flash by. My vision blurs with tears. I wasn't ready for this.

Like a bad dream, I feel as if I'm running in slow motion. When my foot finally hits the first steps of my apartment building I'm frantic to get inside. I reach into my jacket pocket and fish out the keys. With shaky hands, I wrestle with them for a moment before I unlock the door. As I slip inside and turn to shut the door behind me, I scan the street. No one is around. The block is empty. Drunk men weren't chasing me. My imagination got the best of me.

I shut the door harder than necessary and hustle back to my unit. I've had enough excitement for one night. I'm ashamed and angry with myself. Once inside the apartment, I peel out of my coat and make a beeline for the kitchen. Why? I pace back and forth staring down at my feet, mumbling under my breath, "I'm such a stupid girl. I'm a pathetic, scared wimp." The girl I was before still loiters somewhere within. I can't even go outside without having a panic attack. Jake and Vance are dead, but they've won. They laugh at me beyond their graves. I'm at their mercy. Forever.

121

Agitation fills me, bubbling to the surface so that it dances under my skin. It feels like bugs crawling over me. I want to drag my nails over every inch of my body. Am I losing my mind? Desperate for relief, I pull a paring knife from the knife block. I pull the sleeve of my sweatshirt up above my left elbow. Hands shaking, I push slowly, until the sharp point pierces the skin inside my forearm. Cherry-red fluid breaks through and beads up around the steel. I barely feel the sting as the skin splits open and blood trickles down to my elbow. *Yes*. Unsatisfied, I cut three more slices under that one. The last is deeper than the rest and a hiss escapes my lips as the pain sears down to my wrist. In awe, I pause and inspect my handiwork. They run parallel to one another, like rows of a garden. It looks beautiful somehow.

My hands have stopped trembling and the agitation has soothed. Without contemplation, I wash the knife and slip it back into the block on the counter, where it belongs. Relief floods my system and eases the tension in my shoulders. Fatigue creeps in and my thoughts grow murky. I reach for the paper towels and unravel a long bit before wrapping it around my forearm. I'm too tired for anything else. Wandering out of the kitchen and down the hall, my eyes droop heavily.

I think I can sleep now.

CHAPTER FOURTEEN

A shrill racket pierces my wandering thoughts as I stare at the blank wall across the room. I jerk backward, pushing the kitchen chair out and wracking my knee against the table leg. *Shit!* Disoriented, I stand and turn in a circle before I realize it's my smoke alarm going off. *Shit, the eggs.* I turn and bolt to the stove. With a flick of the wrist the burner is off. I toss the skillet to the side. The bottom is scorched and so are my scrambled eggs.

Desperate to stop the ear-piercing commotion, I lean across the sink and throw open the small window. I grab the dishtowel that hangs over the handle of the stove and begin waving it up and down, hoping to fan the smoke out the window. The motion aggravates the scabbed-over cuts on my arm. A knocking at my front door cuts through the ruckus.

Waving my flag, I consider ignoring the door in hopes that whoever is there will give up and leave. They're probably just neighbors wanting to

123

complain about the noise anyway. The alarm stops as quickly as it started, leaving a sharp ringing in my ears.

Another knock echoes through the apartment. *Shit.* "I'm coming." I toss the towel to the kitchen table and scurry down the hall, pulling the sleeves of my shirt all the way down to cover my arm. Just before I reach for the handle, I spot my reflection in the small sun-shaped mirror behind the door. My hair falls out of a messy bun in disarray. My cheeks have a sunken, sallow, zombie-like appearance. I'm wearing the same baggy sweats and sweatshirt I've had on for the past two...no, three days. I grab my sweatshirt and give it a quick sniff. Doesn't smell all that great. I shrug and open the door.

Officer MacGregor stands in front of me in his police uniform. His fresh, clean appearance exacerbates my own uncleanliness. I should have ignored the damn door.

"Umm, hey. Hello."

He cocks one eyebrow. "Miss Benson. Is everything all right?"

"Oh, yeah, just set off the smoke alarm." I giggle nervously, and wipe a strand of hair away from my face. "It's a usual occurrence when I cook. Nothing to worry about." I grasp the doorknob tighter. His presence represents things I'd rather not think about this morning. A muscle under my right eye twitches. "Is there something I can help you with?"

He takes a subtle glance at my outfit. "There have been a few things that have come up with your case and I'd like to ask you a few questions, if that's all right? I tried calling a few times yesterday and then again this morning, but there was no answer. I thought I'd drop by and check up on you. I hope that's okay?"

My mind races. I step back and open the door wider, though I'm reluctant to invite him in. As if sensing my hesitation, he lingers in the hall. Ashamed of myself, I wave my hand in a welcoming gesture. "Please come in. I'm sorry if it smells like burned eggs, but I...well, I got distracted." I look down at my sweats. "And I'm still in my PJs, so if you're okay with that, I'm okay with that." But I'm really not okay with it. He's handsome and I reek. Besides, I'm in no shape for company these days.

A grin spreads over his features like wildfire as he steps inside. "I'm okay with that. You look fine to me."

I shut the door behind him and scurry toward the living room, sniffing the air to see if it smells as bad as I do. Only burnt eggs waft over the air. "Can I make you a cup of coffee?"

"No. I'm fine. Don't go to any trouble. I won't stay long."

I stand by the couch and wait for him to sit on the loveseat before I sit kitty-corner from him.

As he sits, the leather on his gun belt squeaks. His posture is stiff and I wonder if it's the uniform or the topic of conversation that has him so uptight. "It must be uncomfortable to be in that uniform all day."

"Excuse me?"

"The uniform. It looks uncomfortable."

He looks down as if thrown off by my question.

"I guess. I never really thought about it, but yeah, now that you mention it, it's not the most comfortable outfit I own. I'd much rather be in sweats." He gives me an innocent wink.

My skin flushes with embarrassment.

"I'm just teasing," he says. "Breaking the ice and all that."

I offer a smile. "Told you I was still in my pajamas. I wasn't expecting company."

"I know, I know. Like I said before, I'm sorry I popped over here like this but I tried calling multiple times. Your phone goes straight to voicemail like it's off or the battery is dead. I figured it'd be best to drop by and chat with you myself."

"I don't have my phone anymore. I haven't had it since that night." As the words leave my lips, I instantly regret them.

He catches the beat change. "The night you were kidnapped? Do you happen to know when you had it last? Maybe we can locate it."

My eyes wander the apartment. "I know where it's at. I just haven't gone to pick it up yet."

"Miss Benson? Do you mind if I ask where your phone has been this whole time? When we went over the details of that night, you simply said you lost your phone that night."

I sigh. "I did. In my boyfriend's...my ex-boyfriend's car." The look on Tom's face when he paid me a visit at the hospital pops into my mind. I'm not supposed to speak of him. Of us.

"Your ex-boyfriend's car? Miss Benson, you never mentioned anything about a boyfriend or an ex or anything of that sort."

"Yeah, well, that's because we broke up and I don't really want to talk about it. I didn't want to bring it up. He had nothing to do with the rest of that night, so I didn't feel like it was worth mentioning."

"Miss Benson, I understand your concern with remaining discreet, but it really is best if we know everything we can in detail about that night. If your ex saw someone or something that could help lead us to clues that might fill in the gaps, then maybe we could close this case."

"See, that's what's so frustrating about this whole thing. Why is there still 'a case'? The men who kidnapped me are dead. What's left to investigate?"

He pauses as if contemplating how to articulate his next thoughts. "Miss Benson…"

"Would you please stop calling me that!"

"I'm sorry. Would you prefer I call you Tessa?"

I sigh. "No. I mean, yes, you can call me Tessa. I'm sorry, I'm just agitated. I'm not sleeping well lately."

A look of empathy passes quickly. "Tessa, there is still a very thorough investigation in place because it's important that we find out who was willing to pay men like Vance and Jake for these types of films. We have reason to believe they are linked to other cases in the area like it."

"Sheila Weaverton."

He cocks his head to the side. "What makes you say that?"

I shrug. "Nothing in particular."

127

"Did they mention her?"

"No. Not directly. But they did mention 'the last one' and how they had taken care of her quickly so they wanted to make sure to drag mine out. To make it more entertaining. They never said her name, but I knew who they were talking about."

The fact that there was a man who would pay money for my snuff film jolts me back to reality. I'd somehow forgotten that detail. For some reason, I let myself believe that the whole ordeal died with Jake and Vance. It didn't occur to me that there was still an accomplice to my attempted murder out there somewhere. My stomach sours and my mouth waters as I fight a burst of nausea.

"Are you all right? You look pale."

I stand and walk to the kitchen. "I just need some water." I float above the floor as I walk to the sink. I'm worried I might pass out, so I focus on one step and then the other. Without waiting for the water to get cold, I fill and chug a small tumbler. The room steadies. I sense him behind me. I turn.

He stands in the kitchen archway. "You doing okay?"

"Fine. I'm fine." I walk to the kitchen table and plop down at the chair I sat in earlier, when I let my eggs burn. "I just, I guess I didn't think about the fact that there was anyone else out there related to...to my situation. I'm not sure how to process that, or how to feel about it."

"Understandable." He walks toward me. "Can I sit?"

"Of course."

He sits across from me, his gaze direct but

calming. His blue eyes sparkle with genuine concern. "Can I ask who all you interacted with that evening? Maybe if we go over the details of that night, something might come up that didn't seem odd at the time, but seems odd looking back."

I shake my head, reluctant to mull over the details again. "I told you. I did see Vance that night at the club. I remembered him from the library a few days before. Jake was next to him, but I didn't know who he was yet. They're the only ones I remember seeing. No one else seemed to be with them."

His lips purse together in concentration. "Okay, well, who did you talk with that night? Did you run into anyone? Dance with anyone?"

Memories of the incident in Tom's car rush forward, but I don't want to talk about that. "I danced with my ex, Tom, but that was it." I pause, watching his face to see if he believes me. "Oh, and we ran into Gerald that night too, but we didn't really talk."

"Gerald? Who is that?"

With a flick of the wrist, I toss the question aside, as if unimportant. "Oh, he's a guy I was seeing a while back. No big deal."

"Another ex?"

"No. I mean, yeah, I guess. We dated for a couple of weeks, but I wasn't into him. Nice guy. Too nice, probably. Other than him, I really didn't interact with anyone other than Terin. So there's no reason to hash it out again."

"Well, that may or may not be true, which is why I ask all the annoying questions over and over again, because you just never know when something will trigger a thought or idea that leads to a clue. We have no idea how they choose the women they target. Do they know the women? Is it random? We don't know. That said, this all leads me to why I came by in the first place."

My heart stops. Then starts again, thundering like racehorse hooves against my ribcage. "Why? Why did you come by?" I already know the answer.

His blue gaze holds mine. "I know I said I wouldn't ask again but…"

"Then don't."

He sighs and closes his eyes for the briefest of moments before opening them again. "I have to."

I clench my teeth so tight my jaw aches.

"Tessa, I'm sorry, but we need that SD card."

I stand, knocking the chair back abruptly, the legs scraping the floor. "No!"

He stands, his stance wide and firm. "Calm down. I know why you don't want it to get out, Tessa. I understand. I really do. But there might be something, anything that could lead us to whoever buys these films. Don't you see?"

My hands shake so hard I can't hide it, so I jam them into my sweat pockets. I'm torn. I want to catch the asshole behind this whole ugly scheme but I can't bring myself to let that video out to anyone. I can't bear it. "I don't have it," I lie. "I burned it."

"You burned it?" He knows I'm lying. I don't care.

"Yes. I burned it. As soon as I was released from the hospital."

Silence fills the room as he eyeballs me

130

suspiciously. His voice is calm when he speaks, almost a whisper. "Listen, Tessa. I'm here to help you. I want to help you. With your cooperation, we can find this guy and anyone else who could be linked to these crimes. It would give you, and whoever else they've done this to, justice. I want that and I know you want that. But I need your assistance."

Tears spill over. "I can't. I just can't."

His body language softens. He understands. I sense that he wants to offer me comfort but knows I'm not ready to accept it.

"Is there anything I can do for you right now?"

I press my lips tight to stop them from quivering. "No. Thank you. I just need to be alone."

He reaches into his front shirt pocket and pulls out a business card. "If you need anything, I'm serious, anything at all, you call me. If you remember something they said, or a name they mentioned that could prove useful, just call. I'm here for you, Tessa."

I nod. "Okay." *Just leave. Just leave.*

"I'll show myself out."

I nod. When he walks away, I stand, frozen to that spot in the kitchen until I hear the front door close. I wait another minute while I imagine him walking down the hall and out of the building. Then I wait just a bit longer to be sure. When I know he's long gone, I snatch the paring knife, pull up the sleeve on the opposite arm, and carve out matching parallel lines. A sharp hiss escapes my lips with each desperate slice. The pain offers some relief. I'll take what I can get.

CHAPTER FIFTEEN

Standing in front of the display of apples, I try to tune out the myriad of sounds of the local grocery store. I'd never noticed the sheer amount and variety of sounds that assault a person every single day. Lately, I can't un-notice it. I don't like the feeling I get when I'm out in crowds now. Like I'm too vulnerable, like I stick out like a sore thumb. Though when I take a look around, no one even seems to notice I'm there.

My focus returns to the apples. When I pick one up to inspect it, my hands shake. I place the apple back in its place and knock three to the floor. Embarrassed, I scramble to pick them up, worried I'm making a scene. When I finally have the apples stacked, I feel the hot flush of red on my face. I'm not in the mood for this. I just can't do it today. I set my basket on the floor, abandoning the two other items it holds, and rush outside.

All the way home, I curse under my breath, lashing out at my own meek stupidity. Why can't I get my shit together? My hands sweat as I turn off

132

the car and head into my building. My heart stops then restarts when I see a man huddled next to my apartment door. He's hunched over as if he's messing with the lock. He jerks upright and spins on his heel as if he knows he's been caught.

"Gerald?"

A nervous grin flits over his features. He bends and picks up a small bouquet of flowers off the dusty floor. "Tessa. Hello. I brought you flowers."

He takes a step toward me but I stay put. "Flowers? But what were you doing with my door?"

He pauses and looks over his shoulder at the door. "Nothing. I was going to knock, then I thought about just leaving, then I considered just leaving the flowers on the floor by the door. I was nervous about coming by, but I've been following your story on the news, and been so concerned. What an ordeal you've been through. I just had to come by and bring you these. I wanted you to know…well, that I cared."

He holds the flowers straight out, waiting for me to accept them. I'm almost afraid to. With hesitation, I close the gap between us and take the flowers. I hold them to my nose and smell them, as expected, though my mind races. I can't help but wonder what he was doing just before I walked in.

"They smell lovely. It was nice of you to bring them, Gerald."

His grin widens. "I'm glad you like them."

Uncomfortable silence permeates the air. "I'd invite you in but, the place is a mess. I'm not really prepared for company. You know?"

"Oh, of course not. After all you've been

133

through, I'm sure having guests is the last thing on your mind. I won't bother you any further. But do you think, you know, once things settle down, that you might want to have lunch? Or even just a cup of coffee? No strings. Just hang out a little."

I suppress a sigh. He just won't take no for an answer. Does anyone ever listen to anything I say? "Sure, that would be nice. How about I give you a call sometime? We'll set something up."

Brows raise and his eyes light up. "Sounds perfect. So…yeah, just give me a call. No rush." He skirts around me. We do-si-do, swapping places in the hall. I'm not opening my door until he leaves.

"Okay then, good night. Enjoy the flowers."

I nod, willing him to leave at a faster pace. "Good night. Thanks."

I hold my breath as he walks out the door. Then I let it out in a big whoosh and turn to my door. I kneel down and inspect for any signs it's been tampered with. No new scratches. It looks fine. I roll my eyes. I'm out of my mind with paranoia these days. A crazy person. With a fresh dose of shame and guilt, I enter my unit, with fresh flowers tucked under my arm. I'm going to hide away for the rest of the day. Tomorrow is a new day.

***

"You're going back to work already?" Terin hovers in the doorway to my bedroom with a dumbfounded look. "Are you sure that's a good idea?"

Facing my full-length mirror, I avoid eye

134

contact, and wrap a scarf around my neck. I like the way it matches my gray slacks. Unfortunately, the color doesn't do much for my sallow skin. At least the bruising is gone now. Oh, well. "I can't hide in this apartment forever. I've been holed up in here for almost a week. It's time, don't you think?"

She gives a noncommittal shrug. "I mean, I guess. It's just that, you're…"

I stare at her through the reflection in the mirror, giving her my full attention. I'm not in the mood for this right now. "I'm what?"

Her eyes dance in different directions nervously avoiding mine. "I don't know. You're just…"

"I'm just what?"

She looks at me sideways. "Look, I'm just trying to say you've been through a lot and you're not quite yourself yet."

I turn and face her. "Not quite myself? I don't even know what that means. Who am I, Terin?"

A lengthy pause fills the charged air between us.

"What do you mean?"

"Exactly what I said. Who am I? Because I sure as hell don't know anymore."

She shifts her weight back and forth between her feet as if she's thinking of fleeing the scene. "Hey, I'm not trying to upset you. All I'm saying is that it's okay to take some time to regroup before you head back to work. No one is pressuring you to do anything before you're ready."

"Yeah, well, I'm not sure if I'll ever be ready, so I might as well get to it sooner than later. I'm going nuts in this house." The pitch of my voice rises and I know I should calm down, but I can't seem to squelch the rising agitation bubbling inside of me. "In fact, I think I'm flat out going nuts. I mean, I can't eat or sleep. I don't deal with being around people or in public, but I can't just hide away in this damn apartment anymore either." I march past her and down the hall toward the kitchen.

Terin's familiar footsteps shuffle just behind me. "Are you still having trouble sleeping?"

Reaching up into the cupboard I pull down two mugs. "I've slept better, that's for sure."

"And by the looks of things, I'm guessing you're not eating much either."

Shoving one cup under the Keurig, I pop a K-cup in and push start before spinning on my heel to face Terin. "What is this? An interrogation? Should I hop on the scale too? No, I'm not eating or sleeping well. I admit it. Given my recent situation, I don't think it's all that abnormal, right? What do you want me to do? Just hide from the world? I can't do that." I want to do just that.

She shakes her head and takes a step toward me apologetically. "That's not what I'm saying at all. You don't have to be so defensive. Of course it's normal to have trouble after everything you've been through. Shoot, I'd be a freaking mess. All I'm getting at is that the situation is a little above and beyond the norm, so maybe you need a little more time."

A flash of anger and embarrassment surges through me but I squash it, because I know she means well. I turn toward the Keurig and switch the empty mug for the freshly brewed one while I collect myself. I'm sure I probably need a lot more

136

than a counselor, but I have no idea where to begin or what I would even say to one. Self-conscious, I tug at the sleeves of my blouse. If Terin's concerned over a little insomnia and weight loss, it's a damn good thing she can't see my arms right now.

"I don't need more time. I need to get over it, face my fears, and just say fuck it, right? I just need to get back to work and pretend everything is okay."

Terin's eyes are wide, and when she speaks, she talks slowly, as if she is carefully choosing each word, but her tone is firmer than before. "No, it's not okay. None of this is okay. That's my exact point. You shouldn't be heading to work if you're struggling so much to get through this. You need help."

I point to the center of my chest. "Help? I need help? Are you kidding me right now?" I throw a hand in the air, exacerbated. "What kind of help would you suggest for someone like me? Someone who has always been a pushover. Someone who never stands up for herself. Someone who is kidnapped and then murders her captors with her bare hands as a desperate means of survival. Then when she is free, she's not really ever free because now she's a captive of her own fears and delusions. Her own self-punishment. There's not much that can be done for that girl. She's an unsalvageable train wreck. The only thing anyone can do for her is to just stand back and stay out of the way so she doesn't take you down with her."

When I pause, only the sound of my heaving breathing fills the awkward silence between us.

"Is that how you see yourself?" Terin asks. "A

train wreck that everyone should stay away from?"

Anger spikes within my core. I run both hands through my hair and let out a scream. "Why does everyone ask so many questions? Why doesn't anyone ever listen to me?" I plop down on a kitchen chair and cover my face, sobbing into my palms with frustration.

Terin's soft footsteps approach me and she gently lays a hand on my shoulder. I'm afraid to look up and see the expression on her face. I've never lost it so completely in front of anyone before, minus the meltdown in the hospital.

She kneels down and waits for me. After a few minutes of succumbing to the onslaught of tears, I wipe away the salty streaks and snot and finally look her in the face. She smiles faintly. "I'm listening."

Her gentle understanding instigates another wave of tears. This time I reach out and hug her. "I'm sorry. I really am. I'm such a mess and I hate it and don't know what to do about it. I just have so much fear and anger mixed up inside of me and filling my insides that I feel as if I'm drowning from it. I'm just…I'm just lost. You know?"

She pulls away from the hug to look me in the eye. "I don't know, Tess. I really don't. But I want to be here for you and try my best to understand. You have to believe that."

I wipe away the tears and imagine how I must look. I nod. "I know. I do believe that. It's probably the only thing I do believe. You're the only one I trust anymore. I'm sorry I lashed out at you like that."

"It's okay. I'm the only one you have to lash out at. And I probably was hovering too much, asking too many questions. You don't need that right now. You just need support."

I sigh, feeling suddenly drained. "You're probably right. I should see someone. It certainly couldn't hurt. How about, after work, I call around and make an appointment? Would that make you feel better?"

"Anything that makes you feel better, will make me feel better."

I nod and close my eyes, doubtful that I'll ever feel better. "Okay. I'll think about it."

***

Despite my trepidation about returning to work, the serenity of the library envelopes me with open arms and a welcome calm settles over my being. My boss, Gretta, has been gone all morning. I'm staying away from the front desk and hovering back and forth between the back room and sorting incoming books to their shelving on the floor.

During my lunch break, Gretta marches into the employee lounge, which essentially consists of a small round table, a mini fridge, and a cart on wheels with random kitchen items stacked haphazardly. She pauses just inside the doorway, looking down her nose at me with a look of surprise rather than her usual distaste. "I didn't know you'd be here today."

Holding a slice of cucumber in mid-air, I swallow the previous bite nervously. "I would have called to let you know but I...I don't have a cell phone at the moment. I thought it would all right."

Hovering on other side of the room as if scared to get too close, she shakes her head. Her stiff gray hair is sprayed thick with hairspray and refuses to shift or sway with her movement. "It's fine. Just fine. I...wasn't sure you'd be up for it so soon after...after the ordeal you've been through."

I sense fear in her. The look on her face reflects it clearly. When she looks at me she sees someone who survived the unimaginable by committing a horrendous act. Like Terin, she has no idea how to be around me. Her nervous energy triggers my own familiar agitation, so I pack up the remaining food into the Tupperware, and scoot out of the chair. "I'm just finishing here."

Gretta sidesteps to the corner, allowing a wide berth between us as I scurry out of the room. Neither of us says another word.

The rest of the day drags by as I make every effort to avoid other people. Withdrawing into the fearful apprehension of my inner world, I hide away in the back room, surrounded by paperwork. I desperately want to leave early but I refuse. I must get through this test. If I don't, I'm not sure I'll ever be able to return. Why do I feel like this? I'm a survivor. Where is my courage? The bravery that saved my life? How do I get back to that place of strength?

My hands tremble incessantly as I file papers, the battle in my mind consuming me. Imaginings of returning to the confines of my apartment, repress all other thoughts. Silence. Absence of judgment. A

140

paring knife awaits. The scabs on my forearms itch.

CHAPTER SIXTEEN

The muscles in my shoulders relax just a fraction as tension eases with my departure from the library. The memory of meeting Vance out on the front steps surges forward as I walk out the door. I push it down deep and tuck my chin, as if resisting the thought physically too. I'm leaving a half hour early, but in my current state I see this as a win. I made it through the first day back. It wasn't pretty, but it counts. It has to.

Defending myself from the unusually frigid weather, I button my peacoat, then hug myself tightly as I descend the stairs. As I reach the bottom stair, my vision tunnels. I reach for the railing and brace my weight as I fight to remain conscious and standing. I haven't eaten since lunch and that consisted only of half-eaten yogurt and sliced vegetables. Nothing of substance. I need food.

Once desperate to get to my car and back to the sanctuary of home, I'm now focused on eating something, anything, to get my blood sugar up. I can't drive like this. Rather than rounding the corner of the library and heading to my car, I regain composure and walk the opposite direction with hurried steps. There's an Irish pub less than two blocks away.

The streets are busy. Pedestrians rush from point A to point B. It feels as if they're all staring at me. I duck my head and scurry along faster.

Approaching the pub, an African-American teen girl stands in the entryway handing out flyers, hopeful excitement shining brightly from her big brown eyes. I'm shaky and weak. I don't have the energy to deal with people. Even this innocent young girl. Averting my eyes, I keep my head down and brush past her, hoping she'll take the hint and leave me alone.

"Miss?"

No such luck. I ignore her and open the door anyway.

"Miss? Would you like to take a flyer? It's just an advertisement for our new studio down the road. We teach various forms of self-defense and martial arts. You want to protect yourself, don't you?"

As the door swings shut behind me, I stand frozen, my head still aimed at the ground. Her question echoes in my mind. I turn and open the door again, extending my hand. "Sure. I'll take a flyer."

She pauses briefly, a look of pleasant surprise endearing her youthful, round face. "Hey, great!" She licks her finger and thumb and pulls a flyer from the top of the stack. "It's my family's business. We just opened this month and we're excited to get new customers. We have an orientation class tonight if you'd like to show up and take a look at what we have to offer. I think you'd like it."

Her enthusiasm overwhelms me and I wish I wouldn't have turned around. I take the offered flyer, fold it quickly, and tuck it into the front right pocket of my coat. "Thank you. I might do that." Before she can say anything further, I turn and retreat inside the restaurant.

"We'll see you tonight then," she calls out as I walk away.

I shake my head, knowing I won't go out tonight. I'm tired. Scared. A fucking mess. Why did I decide I wanted the flyer in the first place?

***

With a full belly, I walk inside my apartment and shed my coat. As I hang it in the hall closet, I notice the flyer poking up out of the pocket. With a sigh of resignation, I close the door, out of sight. Weary from the day, I shuffle into the living room and flop down onto the couch. I feel strange. Not sure what I'm feeling, exactly. Full. I finally ate more than I've had in one sitting for almost two weeks now. I'm no longer agitated like I was at work, aching for release, but I'm definitely restless. Antsy.

I'm glad to be home. Feels good to have my walls surrounding me. Yet, I'm not satisfied with being alone, doing nothing. I'm bored. I need something to stimulate me. But what? I don't want company, not even Terin. I don't want to leave the house, that's for sure.

I lean forward and pluck the remote from the coffee table. Leaning back in the deep cushions, I prop my feet up on the table and turn on the television. Flip through the channels half-heartedly. Cooking network. Talk shows. News. Weather. I pause for a moment when I come across an old *Friends* rerun. Used to be my favorite show. Still is. Now, for some reason, the antics of the characters and the obnoxious laugh track set my nerves on edge. I continue to scroll through the channels and finally settle on VH1. They're having an Elton John tribute. I close my eyes and listen to the music.

An image of Officer MacGregor sitting in my living room comes to mind. I feel the corners of my mouth turn upward. It feels foreign to smile. The image behind my eyelids reminds me of why he came by that day. The video card. The smile fades and my belly quivers. My brow furrows tight against the onslaught of images that follow, as I imagine what the camera saw from its point of view.

I open my eyes and stare at the ceiling above, my mind racing.

I should watch the video.

This idea both enthralls and sickens me. Can I do it? I leap off the couch and march down the hall to my bedroom. Crouching low, I belly crawl under my bed and reach up under the wooden frame, unable to see what I'm doing. My heart skips a beat when my fingers don't find what they're searching for. Where is it? What if Officer MacGregor broke into my home and found it? That's ludicrous. He needs a warrant. Oh god! What if he comes back with a warrant?

An audible sigh whooshes past my lips as my fingers graze over the small pouch I taped to the underside of one of the supporting frame boards. I wrench it free and scramble out from underneath. With trembling fingers, I unzip it and pull out the SD card. I hate this vile thing.

Before I can change my mind, I rush back down the hall and set everything up so I can stream the footage to my television. Like the horror film that it is. With the remote in hand, I shuffle backward. When my calves hit the edge of the couch, I startle and sit abruptly. I don't know if I can do this.

I have to do this. I hit the power button. The screen comes alive. Push play.

Jake peers directly into the lens, his face filling the entire scene. My vision tunnels. I hit the pause button and fling the remote to the opposite end, stand up, and pace the floor. Blood rushes from my face to my toes. I feel dizzy. I sit back down and stare at the ominous remote. I can't do this.

Breathe in. Breathe out. They're both dead. They can't hurt me. I can watch this. I can.

I hit play and sit on the edge of the couch, my back straight as I wait for what's to come. I hold my breath. Jake comes on the screen. He's mumbling under his breath as he sets up the camera. I can't make out what he's saying but the low tenor of his voice sends shivers down my spine.

The screen goes black, then flickers back on. The room is empty minus the small bed next to the far right wall. I rub my wrists, recalling the way the rope burned. The film freezes, as if it's on pause. I

146

wait, my chest rising and falling with building anticipation. Maybe there is no film to be seen. Maybe there was a mistake. I suppress the urge to let out a laugh as I imagine an alternate scenario where Vance and Jake realize they'd tormented and then killed me only to discover their equipment wasn't working properly and they'd missed the entire thing. A cruel joke.

The screen goes blank again. I stare at the black screen, waiting. I lean back into the couch, afraid to let out a sigh of relief. The screen comes alive. The lighting has changed. The room is darker, with only a faint strain of light streaming through the curtain-less window. Even in the dimmer condition, I clearly see the shape of a woman on the bed, her hands behind her back. Her body is limp. Unconscious.

A thick lump fills my throat, making it hard to swallow. I lean forward, watching the way she sleeps on the screen. She looks so small, so helpless. I want to scream at her, "Get up! Get out of there, you stupid girl!"

But she wouldn't hear me.

I watch for what seems like forever as the clueless girl sleeps. When she finally wakes up and sits on the edge of the bed, she is disoriented. She slowly takes in her surroundings. Skittish eyes dance around the room until they finally look straight into the camera. Her skin pales as terror claims her soul.

With a flick of the remote, I hit pause and once again toss it to the couch. I can't watch what she's about to go through. What I'm about to go through.

That terror. I lived it once, I don't think I can bear to view it remotely. Anger washes over me. Shame flushes through my blood, searing my insides. I want to scream. I want to cut myself again. I can already feel the way the blade will slice through each layer of skin. The way it burns. The relief that follows.

How could I have found myself in such a predicament in the first place? I should have been able to fight them off from the very beginning.

Fight them off.

I shoot a glance toward my front door, then march to the hall closet and yank it open. The flyer for the self-defense class pokes up out of the pocket, still waiting patiently. I pull it out and scan the front. Orientation will start in fifteen minutes. I need this. I don't know why, but I'm suddenly desperate to take this class. I'm tired of being scared. Snagging my coat, I rush out the door, taking only enough time to lock the door behind me.

CHAPTER SEVENTEEN

In the throes of fall, full darkness has settled over the city since well before five o'clock. At ten minutes to seven, it feels more like ten at night. It disorients the senses. I sit in my car, parked half a block from the address on the flyer and consider turning around. The desperation that consumed me earlier has faded. Anxiety has crept in and once again found a home in the center of my chest, where my heart flutters faster and faster. I hate this feeling, loathe it.

Leaning forward, I close my eyes and press my forehead to the steering wheel. Where is the woman who fought for her life by killing two men with her bare hands? She's there somewhere inside me. I know it. She busted through my shy, broken demeanor once, like an unleashed pit bull turned loose in a dog fight. She's there. How do I find her?

Determined to find this girl, I take a quick nervous glance around and make sure it's safe before exiting the car. The streets are busy this time of evening, people still rushing to the store after work, or to dinner, or maybe to see their lovers. Everyone lost in their own self-absorbed lives, oblivious to anyone else's struggles or plight. Nothing seems out of the ordinary, so I slide out of the driver's side and dart around the front of the car to the curb.

On the sidewalk, I pause long enough to look up at the clear sky. My breath plumes out in a puff of fog. The night air is unusually frigid, singeing my nose hairs. I wrap my scarf around the lower half of my face so that my nose and mouth are covered, then head toward the end of the block.

As I approach the building, it seems quiet. I pull at the silver handle but the overly large door won't budge. It's locked. I take a step back and recheck the address to make sure I have it correct. It's then that I notice the yellow piece of paper taped to the unassuming sign on the side wall of the building.

'STUDENTS: PLEASE ENTER THROUGH THE SIDE DOOR TO THE RIGHT OF THE BUILDING.'

Under the bold writing is a large red arrow pointing to the right.

I look to the right and see two women walking side by side in my direction, then turn the corner. They giggle in unison, carefree and whimsical on a cold night. They don't know danger or fear. Heat swirls in my belly. I'm jealous of them. Resentful, even. I shouldn't be here, but I refuse to leave. I have to at least check it out or I'm just going to go home and carve new brutal marks into my flesh while the remainder of my video awaits, eager to be watched.

With images of the video fresh in my mind, I follow the women and wait until they are inside for a moment before entering. The door is heavy. I pull it open and slip in. Bright lights and warm air embrace me. My heart races as I realize I'm in a large studio filled with random strangers. They gather in various circles, socializing and getting to know one another before the orientation begins. Everyone is dressed in workout-type clothing. I glance down at my own outfit. Under my pea coat, I'm still wearing my work clothes and one-inch heels. I stick out like a sore thumb. I don't belong here.

I spin on my heel to make a quick exit and run smack into a tall male form. Eye level to his chest, I notice he's broad shouldered and muscular under the long-sleeved nylon workout shirt he's wearing. He smells good too.

I take a step back. "I'm so sorry. I didn't mean..."

"Well, hello, Miss Benson. It's good to see you here."

I sputter to find the right words. "Officer MacGregor. What...what are you doing here?"

He smiles wide to flash his perfect teeth. "I've been asked to help with the orientation tonight. I know the family who runs it quite well. In fact, I've been training with them for years, and I'm excited that they're finally able to open their own gym. I'll be helping with some of the classes."

"Oh, I see." Now I know I definitely can't do this. I need to get out of here but don't know what

151

to say. Should I just run out of the building? "I didn't recognize you at first in civilian clothes."

"Yeah, I've heard that before. I think it's that way for anyone who wears a uniform. It looks odd when they're out in public wearing regular clothes. I'm glad to see you here, though. You gonna take a class?"

Laughing nervously, I'm racking my brain on how to get away without being rude. "No. Um, well, I thought about it, but…"

"But what?"

I shake my head and look away. More people are filing inside. It's too crowded. The walls are closing in.

"Tessa?"

The lilt in his tone begs me to look his way. Gradually, I lift my gaze to his. His blue eyes pierce through the barriers I'm trying to keep up around me. It's too much. "I'm sorry, but I have to go." I bolt toward the door.

"Tessa, no, wait!"

His large hand grasps me by the shoulder, and without thinking I turn and swipe it away with one brisk and fluid motion. He puts his hands up in defense. "It's okay. Just please don't go yet."

Surprised by my own reaction, I'm speechless. "Why?"

He lowers his voice to almost a whisper. "Because, I think it will be good for you. You need this. You've been through a lot and I know you're struggling. This could help you get your life back."

"What life?" The words are out before I can stop them. I glance around to see if anyone is watching

152

our exchange. Officer MacGregor watches me patiently.

"Look, stay for the orientation. Then, at the end, if you never want to come back, that's fine. Please stay. For me."

His eyes plead with me. I remember the time I asked him to stay with me in the hospital. And he did. Why does he care if I stay? Is it that obvious I'm such a damn mess? I can't summon the words to deny him. "Fine. I'll stay. But just for the orientation. That's it."

A beaming grin brightens his face. "Good! Now, follow me and we'll get you a good place to hang out so you can see everything."

Still uncomfortable, I allow him to steer me to the opposite side of the room where a large mat covers the floor. "Stand just off the mat. Feel free to sit if you want. There are chairs along the wall. We're about to get things started, so I'll see you around."

"Okay." Despite the fact that he has made a spot for me up front, I trickle through the crowd and find a chair in the back corner. I feel better here, out of the way. A short, stout African-American man walks to the center of the room and introduces himself. Conversations hush as everyone finds a seat.

He looks familiar. When he introduces his daughter, it clicks. It's the girl who passed out the flyers. I'd forgotten she said it was a family business. I wonder how Officer MacGregor came to be involved with them.

As they start explaining their history and how

they have passed along their business of training self-defense throughout multiple generations, I slowly relax. They introduce Officer MacGregor and offer a vague explanation of how they've known him for many years and he's become like family. I sense there is a story here and I'm curious to learn more.

It occurs to me that I could probably sneak out the back door while they're talking and they'd never notice. I clutch my purse, toying with the idea. Officer MacGregor and the main instructor start sparring with one another. Their moves are short and quick, precise. They move with a strength and agility that catches my breath. It's beautiful. I'm captivated. Flashes of those brief moments when I had executed my own graceful violence blow through my mind.

They bring up volunteers and walk them through a few basic moves. A few of the volunteers catch on quick. They beam with pride. A fire has been lit inside them.

I want that. I want that fire.

A few times throughout the demonstrations, Officer MacGregor searches the room and I know he's looking for me. When he finally spots me, the corners of his mouth turn up a fraction and he gives me a nod. I pray that he won't call me to the front as a volunteer. I don't think he will. He knows I'm not ready for that.

By the end of the class, I'm hooked. I need this outlet. I'm nervous that I will suck, but I want this more than anything I've wanted in a long time. I wait in the back corner while the crowd slowly filters out of the room. Officer MacGregor catches my eye and marches in my direction. I meet him in the middle.

He wears a smile but his brow is raised in question. "Well? What do you think?"

"Teach me."

"I was hoping you'd say that," he answers, his expression humorless. "But only if you promise to call me Tobin from now on."

"Tobin. Fine. When can we start?"

He laughs. It's warm, sensuous. "So eager, suddenly. I'm glad. I think it will be good for you." He looks around the room, then guides me off to the side with a light touch to the elbow. His voice lowers. "Hey, I wanted to apologize again for dropping in on you the other day so unexpectedly. I know I upset you, and I've been feeling terrible ever since."

I'm looking at his hand on my elbow rather than up into his face. I shrug. "It's fine."

He bends down and peers at me until I cave and look directly into his eyes. They reflect the sincerity of his apology. I offer a thin smile. "It really is okay."

He straightens to his full height. "Good. I'm glad to hear I'm forgiven. Also, when our conversation took a turn, I forgot to ask the names of the men you'd spoken to that night. Your exes? I believe you said one of them was Tom?"

Frustrated at the fact that he has high-jacked the conversation and squelched the rare feeling of excitement I'd experienced about the self-defense class, I roll my eyes and look away. "Do we have to

155

talk about this here? Now?"

His body language softens. "Of course not. You're right. I'm sorry. Maybe we can talk later this week. I could come by on the way home from the station?"

Cocking my head to the side, I give him a sideways glance. I'm not sure how I feel about him coming by my house, digging at me again with more questions. Yet, I trust him, and he's just doing his job. "Okay, sure. That would be fine. Not tomorrow, but anytime Thursday or Friday would work."

A grin encompasses his features and washes away the little bit of frustration I'm feeling.

"Great! So you'll be at class tomorrow then?"

"Uhhh…"

"Come on. Don't be shy. You were totally excited a few minutes ago."

I nod. "Yeah, yeah, I'll come to tomorrow's class then. I'll even bring a friend."

***

"Thanks for coming with me," I say to Terin as she waits anxiously on the edge of the mat. "It's my first official class and I'm nervous. I'm afraid I'm going to back out."

"Are you kidding me? A room full of sweaty men? I wouldn't miss it for the world."

"It's hardly a room full of sweaty men, Terin. They're mostly women. There might be four men total, if that. And they're nothing special to look at. Kind of small, meek men who need to learn to defend themselves, if you know what I mean. If you're looking for hot, sweaty men, this might not be the place for it. Try the 24 Hour Fitness down the street."

"Yeah, well, it's not like I can do this all the time anyway. I'm not exactly the workout kind of girl, ya know. I like to keep my assets soft." She giggles hysterically, clearly amused by her own humor. She snorts and slaps my shoulder. "Holy mother of God, woman! You lied. That man right there is delicious."

I turn in the direction she gestures with her chin, anticipating who I'll find at the end of her comment. Sure enough. Tobin walks from across the room and onto the mat. He's wearing sweats and a snug t-shirt that reveals his muscular build. He walks with confidence, but he's not cocky. His hair is tousled as if he's already been sparring before class. I swallow down a nervous giggle.

"Yeah, well he's the instructor. And he's a cop. The one from my case. Remember? He was at the hospital."

Her eyebrows raise and her eyes light up. "Well, dang if it isn't him. I didn't recognize Officer Hotty McHotterson out of his police uniform. He looks just as good in baggy sweats, if you ask me."

I avert my gaze because I don't want him to catch us checking him out. "Yeah, he's all right."

"All right?" She slaps me again. "Come on, woman. I know you've been through a lot lately but your hotness radar hasn't died off. Don't tell me you don't think he's a babe."

I shake my head and suppress a smile. "I wish I

157

hadn't brought you. I can't take you anywhere."

We laugh in unison. I'm grateful for Terin's off-beat humor.

"Besides, we had a deal."

I sigh. "Yeah, I know. Don't remind me."

"Hey, girl. Don't roll your eyes at me. A deal's a deal."

"Yeah, but a support group?"

Terin's body language shifts as she turns to face me head on. Her tone drops so that no one will overhear our conversation but there is no doubting the gravity of her earnestness. "Yes, a support group. For women who have survived trauma."

"But it's for battered women."

"Not just battered women. It's for any woman who has survived violence. Yeah, there will be a lot of battered women there, but there will be an array of other women there who need support too. You'll be one of many. And I'm sorry, but you need it. No matter how hard you try to act like you're okay, I'm your best friend and I know you're nowhere near okay. Soooo you're going. You promised."

I roll my eyes again for effect. "Yeah, yeah, yeah. A deal's a deal. I'll go. Now let's learn to kick some butt from Officer McHotty."

She giggles and rubs her hands together earnestly. "Oh, yeah. A deal's a deal."

CHAPTER EIGHTEEN

Google Maps shows that the support group meeting is only five blocks east, then two blocks south of my apartment. I weigh my options. Do I want to walk or drive? Seems ridiculous to drive that short distance, but I can't stand the anxiety that overwhelms me whenever I have to go out in public these days.

Parking is atrocious in that area of town. Not to mention the annoyance of dealing with one-way streets. Forgoing the option of driving, I snag my keys and umbrella, lock up, and head out. The meeting starts at five thirty, so I'd better get going before I let the nagging anxiety take over and make an excuse not to go. Why did I promise Terin I'd do this?

When I step out into the fresh air, I open my umbrella against the thin dusting of mist that hangs in the air. Daylight Saving Time has darkness settled over the city and streetlights shining down. I shiver against the cold and second-guess my decision. I take one last look at the print out to confirm the address before I tuck it in my pocket. When I look up, I notice a man sitting in a car next to the curb. He's got his head tipped down as if he's looking at something in his lap. The engine is off. I saw him in the same spot two days ago and thought nothing of it. I figured he was picking someone up. Now, something feels off about his presence. A sense of déjà vu sends goosebumps over my flesh. I shake it off and march down the street. I'm paranoid. It's just a man waiting for someone. Maybe a woman in the neighborhood. Maybe a friend.

The eerie sensation of dread lingers with me all the way to my destination. When I find the building, I almost laugh out loud. It's the quintessential gloomy, desolate, rundown building. This is where battered woman seek solace and support? How depressing.

Another wave of doubt washes over me. I could turn around right now and go back home. Terin would never know. I glance around to take in my surroundings. Does anyone notice my struggle? Pedestrians file by. Drivers focus on their commute from work to wherever it is they're going— oblivious to what I'm doing, of course. I could definitely leave and no one would know, or care.

A deal's a deal. Terin's chipper voice echoes in my mind. Guilt follows. I sigh and fold up my umbrella as I stomp up the stone stairs. I strain to open the weighty metal door. When I slip inside, the murmur of hushed voices echoes down the long expanse of hallway. The sound is hollow and sad. This is the last place people who are seeking answers should be.

I keep my chin tucked and eyes averted when I enter the room, hoping to avoid drawing attention in my direction. A fold-out table against the far left wall bears snacks, a carafe of water, and a steel coffee dispenser. A circle of chairs fills the center of the room while a cluster of women huddle in various groupings.

They look so...normal.

I'm not sure what I had been expecting, but it clearly wasn't this. No one has a black eye or fat lip. No one has sunken cheekbones or frail, broken body language. They are average everyday women. Businesswomen, stay-at-home moms, PTA members. Some are young, others middle-aged, and one appears to be a bit more elderly. I feel ashamed that I had stereotyped this group before I'd even laid eyes on them.

"Hello." A soft, curious lilt comes from behind me.

I turn. A petite, bright-eyed woman stares at me expectantly. I offer my right hand. "Oh, hello. I'm Tessa Benson."

"Glad to meet you, Tessa. I'm Shirley Aldrich. I'm the chairperson for our little group here. We're happy to have you join us tonight. Is this your first support group session?"

I nod, glad for her welcoming presence. "Yes, it is. And I'm a bit nervous. I'm not sure this is the right place for me, but a friend insisted I come."

Her eyes crinkle deeply in the outside corner as she smiles with hidden wisdom. "Yes, well, our friends often know what we need and where we should be much sooner than we do. Do you know anything about our group? Do you have any questions before we get started?"

"Umm, my friend said it was a support group for battered women."

Her lips purse as she slowly nods her head. "Well, sort of. It's not specifically just for women who are in abusive relationships, though we certainly have those as well. The more broad-spectrum focus of our group is for women who have survived violence. Of any nature. If your friend thinks you belong here, then it's likely you do. Yes?"

A survivor of violence. Yes, I guess I qualify, though I still don't feel like this is a good fit for me. "I guess."

She smiles. "You just join us for tonight's meeting and you can decide for yourself if this is something that could be of use to you. That's what really matters. In the meantime, I can introduce you around if you like?"

"No. No, thanks. I'll just hang back and get a feel for things, if that's all right with you?"

"Of course, make yourself comfortable. There are drinks and snacks over there. I will, however, ask you to give a brief introduction of yourself when we begin. Is that going to be okay with you?"

My insides cringe. "Yes, I think I can manage that."

"Good, then go ahead and get something to drink. We'll start in a few minutes."

"Thank you."

Instead of heading toward the drink table, I

decide to find a spot in the circle to sit. I have no idea what else to do. I hang my jacket over the back and slide my umbrella under my chair, then fold my hands in my lap and wait patiently for the next hour to pass as quickly as possible.

Shirley approaches the circle of chairs and sits directly opposite me. Soon the rest of the crowd follows suit and the majority of the chairs are filled within minutes. Multiple pairs of inquisitive eyes fixate on me.

"Welcome, everyone," Shirley says with enthusiasm. "Good to see all of you. We have a new face among us so, as we've done in the past, we'll go around and offer a brief introduction of ourselves one at a time so that our guest feels comfortable. I'll start first." She straightens her back and clasps her hands together in her lap, like a school teacher preparing to address her class.

"My name is Shirley Aldrich. I was born and raised here in the Pacific Northwest, mainly the lower Seattle area. I began my work as a social worker about thirty-five years ago, back when I had a lofty idea that I was going to save the world one person at a time. Then real life happened and things were uglier in the real world than I could have imagined. Social work was brutal and exhausting. It sucked the life out of me." Both her tone and body language alter slightly, offering a darker inflection to her story.

"One day while I was on a house call to investigate yet another case of child neglect, I wound up face to face with an extremely angry father who was high as a kite on amphetamines and had no intention of letting me leave his home that day. After the way I found his home and the degree that his two-year-old was suffering from malnourishment, he must have known I would call the police. He refused to let me leave. Things escalated when I tried to escape. I was able to call 911 but he beat me within an inch of my life as a consequence. All I remember after that is the sound of the child as he whimpered in his crib. The sound of sirens surrounding the building. He held me hostage for over twenty-four hours before a SWAT team finally rescued both me and the baby—but not before they shot and killed the father." She pauses. The class is silent, waiting for her to continue.

"Long story short, PTSD is a real thing, and though the incident was over, I suffered the long-term effects of that kind of trauma for many, many months. Eventually, I sought out support groups. I found a lot that focused on battered wives, but nothing that was more generalized to other survivors of violence. So I created my own support group to include a wider group of women who needed support."

The group gives a short round of clapping. Then one by one the rest of the group begins to tell their stories. One woman is the survivor of a mini-mart robbery. She was the cashier on the night shift. The next three women are survivors of long-term abusive marriages. One is still married to her husband, who is in prison. Then a rotund Hispanic woman sitting next to me tells the story of how she was kidnapped at age fourteen by an estranged uncle. She was beaten and raped for two weeks before the police found her. The uncle was killed last year by another inmate while he served time for a different count of rape.

As the room offers their obligatory round of supportive applause, I ponder why we're clapping. These are atrocities we're talking about. Ugliness and violence. It causes cognitive dissonance within me to clap in response to these stories. A scuffle from behind me draws the attention of everyone in the room. I turn to see what's causing the ruckus.

"Sorry, everyone. Sorry I'm late." A tall, burly woman bustles into the room like a long-horned beast breaking through the crowd at a running-of-the-bulls event. She retrieves the cigarette that dangles from her mouth haphazardly and squashes it on the floor, as if we're outside in the dirt. She pulls the hood of her dark blue sweatshirt off her head to reveal dark hair pulled back into a long, thick braid. Strands of gray are woven throughout.

I take in a sharp breath when I spot the deep blue-and-yellow tinted bruise surrounding her left eye. This is what I had expected when I first arrived.

The dynamic of the room shifts immediately as everyone makes room for her to join the circle. Some look apprehensive. Others seem indifferent. I sense she has a strong influence over the group. She makes me nervous.

Shirley offers a welcoming smile. "Glad you could make it, Grace. We were just—"

"Yeah, yeah, yeah," Grace says as she lifts her left leg and swings it over the chair before she plops down in it dramatically. "I'm here. Whatever. Let's not make a fuss…" She stops mid-sentence as her gaze locks on to me. "Well, well, I see we have a newbie. At least that's interesting."

Her smirk is almost a sneer. I shift nervously in my seat and offer a tentative smile.

"This is Tessa," Shirley says. "We were just about to let her introduce herself to the group before you came barreling in."

Grace's eyes are still locked on to mine. Her sneer shifts slowly as recognition lights up her features. Her brows rise. "Hey, I know who she is. I saw her face on the news a crap-ton of times. Yeah, she's the girl who killed those snuff-film fuckers."

The blood drains from my face. I shake my head but I'm not even sure why.

She laughs and nods vehemently, clearly pleased with her discovery. "Oh, yes, you are. You're her. Man, you really showed those fuckers who was boss, didn't you?" She leans forward, both elbows on her knees, a glisten in her eyes. "Tell us how you did it."

Now the entire circle is focused on me, like a group of vultures. *Is that you? Are you the one who did that? Tell us about it. Weren't you scared? What did they do to you?*

I feel both hot and dizzy at the same time. Their barrage of questions overwhelms me and I don't know what to do, so I jump to my feet, scramble to retrieve my umbrella from under the seat, and run out of the room. Shirley calls my name. I ignore it and flee down the hall and out of the building. I'm not ready for this yet.

***

Thursday and Friday come and go with no sign of Tobin after work. I can't decide if I'm relieved or disappointed. I can't decide if that indecision infuriates me or intrigues me. But when a knock echoes through my apartment first thing Saturday morning, I instantly sense that it's him.

I hover in the hallway, pondering whether I should answer or ignore it and wait for him to leave. Guilt vetoes my need to hide, so I open the door.

Tobin stands in the hallway. Dressed in jeans and a hoodie, he looks less formidable than he does in his uniform, but his wide shoulders and sexy confidence still make it appear that he's larger than he is. He seems to fill the space no matter where he is. Like the environment around him is too small for his presence. I find it comforting. Safe, somehow.

He takes in my appearance of running shoes, yoga pants, and rain coat. "You on your way out?"

"Yeah, I was about to go for a run."

His eyes light up. "Oh, yeah? I didn't know you were a runner."

"Well, I was in high school. Cross country. But to be honest, I haven't run much in years. Just too busy, or lazy—both, I guess. Anyway, since the class, I realized how out of shape I am and figured I'd best get back into it. It'll help, don't you think?"

"Certainly. Builds muscle and stamina. It's a great way to supplement the training."

We both fall silent, an awkward pause lingering between us.

"Do you want to come in?" I finally offer

167

stupidly.

"Uh, well, I don't want to keep you from your run. I was just on the way to run some errands, and since I was too busy this last week to come by, like we discussed, I figured I'd see if you were around this morning. I hate to drop in, though. Still no phone?"

My cheeks flush. "No. No phone yet. Guess I should get back to the twenty-first century and get one soon. It's kind of odd, but I haven't missed it. You know?"

As if on cue, his phone pings, notifying him of a message. He gives a sheepish shrug. "Oh, don't I know it. Hey, look, I just came by because we found out the name of the person who owns the cabin, and also, I wanted to get the names of those men. Just to cover all bases."

I grip the door knob tighter. "The cabin? A name?" I sound breathless, even to my own ears.

He gives a single nod, watching my reaction carefully. "Yeah, we think the name is just an alias, because we have yet to actually find anyone under that name, but I wanted to know if the name Benjamin Ashford rings any bells?"

Pressure builds within my skull as I mentally scroll through my name index. I'm not sure if I want to recognize the name or not. I bite my bottom lip and shake my head. "No. No, I don't recognize that name. Someone could have bought the property under another name?"

"Oh, sure. It happens all the time. It shouldn't, but it does. People figure out ways to cheat the system. Especially if there's cold, hard cash

168

involved, which there likely was."

I run the name over and over again through my mind. Still nothing comes up.

He shrugs. "No worries. We'll get it figured out. In the meantime, why don't you give me the names of those men at the club and we'll go from there."

"Sure, sure. So...let's see...I ran into Gerald Snowden that night. He and I went out off and on for about two months. Like I said, nice guy. He liked me a lot more than I liked him, unfortunately. We didn't really talk that night. I ran into him and then pretty much avoided him for the rest of the evening."

Tobin has already reached into his back pocket and retrieved a small notepad. He scribbles quickly, mumbling under his breath as he repeats about half of what I'm saying. When I pause, his head snaps up, waiting in anticipation. "So, why were you avoiding him? Did you two break up amicably or was there strife? Was he upset or disgruntled?"

I hesitate. "I don't think he was happy about it. He continued to make amends afterward, but...look, Gerald's harmless. I'm not worried about him."

"Okay, okay. Well, what about the other guy? Tom, was that his name?"

"Yes, Tom Hastings the Third."

He furrows his brow. "Hastings? Tom Hastings? I know him."

"You do?"

He leans against the doorway with a whimsical look on his face. "Yeah, he and I go way back. Went to college together. Same fraternity and everything. Haven't seen him in quite a while, but yeah, he and I share some stories, that's for sure. Huh, so you and he were a thing?" His tone has a nostalgic tenor mixed with sudden interest.

I shake my head, uncomfortable with the way the conversation has turned. "No, not really a thing. I mean…we went out a few times. I liked him and all that, but he was busy, you know with work…and he, he just didn't have time for a girlfriend. I don't know. We didn't know each other all that long. It wasn't a big deal."

I shift my weight back and forth as he gauges my reaction, his profession seeping into our interaction. The investigator in him taking over.

"But you and he interacted that evening? Any friction between you two?"

The way Tom shoved his cock into my mouth, forcing my head down while I cried salty tears, comes flooding back. "No, not really." I chew on my lip as I mentally chew on the next question. "So…you two are friends?"

He shrugs. "Well, I mean we were. A long time ago. I guess we technically still are, but I haven't seen him in years. How long were you and he a thing? If you don't mind me asking?"

I wonder if he's asking from a personal or professional standpoint. "We weren't really a thing. Like I said before, we only dated for a few weeks. Nothing serious."

"Hmm, okay, well, are you sure you didn't talk with anyone else that night? Or even that week? I know you said that Vance approached you in front of work, at the library. Anything else you can think of?"

I'm done with this conversation. The fact that Tobin knows Tom, even was friends with him in the past, doesn't sit well with me. "Nope. Not that I can think of."

He nods his head, his eyes roaming the hallway, while he processes the conversation. "Well, maybe I'll get in touch with Tom. See if he saw anything odd that night. It'd be good to catch up with him anyway. I'll get out of your hair now." He tucks his pen and notebook into a pocket.

I bite nervously on my bottom lip while fighting the urge to scratch at the scabs on my arms. As he turns away, panic rises within my chest and I reach out toward him. "Actually…"

He stops mid-turn, his head cocked to the side, anticipating my next sentence. "Yeah?"

I pull my arm back in protectively against my chest. "Well, you see…Tom and I…well…we weren't really public about our…relationship, if you can even call it that."

"So, it was a secret?"

Heat flushes my system as shame wells up. "No. Not really a secret. I did tell my best friend Terin about him. But Tom was more private. He didn't want anyone to know anything about his private life. He never even invited me to his home. And I don't want him to know I told you."

His gaze narrows speculatively. "Hmm, that's odd. Doesn't sound like the loud, gregarious Tom that I knew back in college. Did you think he had something to hide, like maybe a wife, or something?"

I shrug. "You know, I'm really not sure. I mean,

171

I did wonder, but I think he's just busy and doesn't want…" I pause before repeating Tom's words out loud. "…a fling."

Tobin purses his lips together as if suppressing the next thought. I know what he's thinking. Tom's a cheater. And maybe he is. All I know is that I don't want Tobin snooping around in my private life anymore, especially when it comes to Tom.

"Look," Tobin says cautiously. "I won't seek Tom out and start asking him a bunch of questions because I can see you're clearly concerned about that. It sounds like a private matter between the two of you and I don't really think it impacts this case in any way. I know Tom. He's a good guy. His personal life is his own business and so is yours. But if you think of anything else that happened that night or even that week before, that didn't seem right, a random stranger approaching you, anything at all, just get in touch with me. Okay?"

"Of course.*" Just leave.*

We say goodbye, an odd tension lingering between us. I close the door and lean against it, my mind frazzled. Will Tobin keep his promise to not talk with Tom about us? Being Tom's secret makes me feel dirty. Like I need a bath. A surge of anger washes over me, replacing the shame. I push off the door and grab my rain jacket. I need to run. Fuck Tom. Fuck everyone.

I lock up behind me and dart out of my building. The rain has stopped but the air is damp and heavy on my face. It's bitter cold too. I welcome it.

Feeling as if someone is watching me, I glance around as I near the bottom stair. Right, left, then

172

right again. Across the street, even up in the windows of the building directly on the other side. Nothing seems out of place. Ignoring the way the hairs stand up on the back of my neck, I break into a run, desperate to shed this growing agitation.

CHAPTER NINETEEN

A strong arm wraps around my waist as something sweeps both of my feet out from under me. The breath is knocked from my lungs in a painful whoosh when my back hits the mat with a dull thud.

"You have to keep your opponent directly in front of you at all times, Tessa." Tobin peers down at me, kneeling by my side. His expression is earnest, minus the hint of a smirk at the right corner of his mouth. "The moment you let someone come at you from the side, you're done."

Catching my breath, I try to ignore both the pain between my shoulder blades and the way my heart beats faster when he's so close to me. I don't care for either. "Yeah, well, that's easy for you to say. You've got what, seventy-five, eighty pounds on me?"

"That's true." He pauses. His eyes gently take me in. I can't breathe. His masculine scent of sweat intermingled with cologne teases me. He's about to say something that will alter our dynamic forever. I sense it. I reach up and place a hand on his chest as if warning him to keep his distance. He glances down and his expression falters. I know what he sees before he says anything. *Fuck.*

I roll away, then scramble to my feet to put more space between us. I shove my shirt sleeves over my forearms, then brush the bangs from my face, hoping he'll ignore what he just discovered.

Still on his knees, he leans back and sits on his heels. "What happened to your arm?"

I sigh. "Nothing. It's nothing."

"It doesn't look like nothing."

My eyes dart toward the other instructor and student on the other side of the gym, hoping they can't hear our conversation even though our voices are hushed.

"Look at me."

Reluctantly, I give him my attention.

"Why do you come here every other night, Tessa?"

"What do you mean?"

He takes a step closer. "I mean you come here and train with me. You work hard. You push yourself. You're learning fast and excelling in training. But why? I think I know why, but I want you to tell me."

"I…I don't know."

"Yes, you do." His brow is set, determined.

"But I don't."

"Yes, you do."

"Because I'm scared!" I yell.

Shocked by my own reaction, I glance again toward our other gym members who are now staring

175

at us with wide-eyed, startled expressions.

"Don't worry about them. Look at me."

My heart gallops in my chest as I turn back to Tobin. "I come because this is the only place I feel safe. It's the only time when I feel like I'm somewhat in control of my life. Every other moment is spent just trying to breathe. I would like to be able to walk down the street without thinking someone is following me. Without being scared out of my mind. Without self-doubt determining my every waking moment."

His expression softens. "Why do you think someone is following you?"

My face contorts with confusion. "What? I can't keep up with you. What are we talking about here?"

"I know what you've been through. How much you've suffered. But you never show it. Not really. I've been wondering how to talk to you, how to get you to open up that shell of yours. And then I see your arms, and it's obvious you're not coping nearly as well as I'd hoped. But now I want to know why you think someone is following you."

"I don't. I mean, I do…sometimes…but that's not the point. I have all kinds of crazy thoughts these days. I don't know if I'm coming or going. I survived something horrible. I killed two men. Yet, I can barely stand to leave my house. I'm losing my mind."

"You did what you had to do to survive. It was instinct. It was desperation. But it was bravery too. That's what you're still not seeing. Even after weeks of training, three nights a week. You still don't see it. You may be scared, but you're brave

176

too. And if you honestly think someone is following you, then I need to know that. I can give you protection. I can make sure you're safe until we find the man who hired your kidnappers."

I cock my head to the side and gauge his sincerity. "You think someone could actually be following me? Maybe I'm not just paranoid?"

He gives a light chuckle. "After all you've been through? No, you're not paranoid."

Silence falls between us. A wave of stifling heat flushes over my body. The scabs on my arms start to itch. It feels good to have someone validate my fears, but in another sense it's absolutely terrifying. I turn and walk to the edge of the mat, snagging my sweatshirt off the floor.

"Where are you going? We still have fifteen minutes left."

I offer him a brief glance, but can't hold it for fear of allowing him to see my growing anxiety. "I'm not feeling well. I'm done for tonight."

"Tessa, wait." He runs to the opposite side of the room to dig through a black backpack. When he returns, he has a yellow sticky note in his hand. "This is my cell phone number. If anything comes up, I don't care what it is, someone looks suspicious, you hear a funny noise, doesn't matter, you give me a call. I'm here for you."

I stare at his outstretched hand for a few brief moments of contemplation before I reach out and take the note. "Thanks." I turn and walk as fast as I can out of the gym.

After lingering in the locker room for what seems like forever, hoping I won't run into anyone and have to be social on the way out, I decide to head home. It's quiet in the hallway, but the lights are still on in the gym, so I slink by and sneak out the back door.

Rain is pouring down in sheets. It's as if the sky has opened up and unleashed its fury. Swearing under my breath, I hide under the thin eave and wrestle my way into my sweatshirt. With my hood pulled over, I duck my head and dart around the building to my car. My foot slips on the slick cement. My arms flail out as I stagger-step to regain my balance. Still upright, I'm more careful with my footing as I rush to the car. Not that it will matter. The icy rain is already soaking through to my skin.

As I approach the curb, I reach into the front pocket of my hoodie for my keys and find only lint. *Shit.* I turn and scan the sidewalk to see if they fell out on the way. Nothing but a crushed latté container lying in a puddle. Tracing my steps, I head back to the gym. I'm surprised to see the main overhead lights are now off. Only the hallway lights filter in through the doorways. An odd sense of disappointment fills me as I realize Tobin is already gone. Why does this make me sad? I just ran from him in humiliation.

Baffled and disgruntled, I scurry across the empty gym, over the mats, and through the nearest opening into the brightly lit hall. The squeak of my wet sneakers bounces off the walls as I make my way to the locker room. I push the door open and breathe a sigh of relief when I spot my keys lying on the bench by the locker I'd used tonight. Thank god.

I snatch them and hurry out the door. Something about being here when everyone else has left gives me the creeps. Then again, I know someone has to be here still because the building hasn't been locked up for the night yet. That thought doesn't make me feel any better, so I pick up the pace.

When I shove the back door open again and step into the night, I'm pleased to find that that rain has stopped. The door thuds closed behind me and I tip up my face toward the sky. I take in a cleansing breath. Nothing smells better than Washington air after a rain.

The sounds of an argument interrupts my brief reverie. I clutch my keys tight to stifle any sound that might signal my presence. Voices of a man and a woman echo down the alley. Goosebumps raise over my flesh and I tuck my hair behind one ear so I can hear them better. Traffic down the road muffles out the details. I can't make out their words, but their tone is angry and threatening. My inner voice whispers, *turn around and mind your own business.*

My heart beats wildly in my chest. I want to listen to that persistent little voice and turn and escape to my car. But something pulls at me. Maybe it's the way the man's tone barks and bullies. Maybe it's the way the woman's tone cajoles and cowers. Trying to soothe the bear. I can't help myself. I tiptoe along the edge of the wall, then peek around the corner. They're about twenty yards away, just in the shadows of the building, away from the streaming beam of the streetlights, amidst what appears to be a small construction project. Long and short two-by-fours are stacked neatly in

179

rows, organization amongst chaos. One wall of the building behind the gym is torn away.

Among the mess, a man and woman face one another in a standoff, not even a foot apart. He towers over her small frame with a finger jutted in her face. Though she's in the shadows, I recognize her from class. She had been the other student tonight.

Just back away. It's none of my business. *Breathe in. Breathe out.* I'm screaming on the inside. *Leave. I need to leave. Just walk away.* I feel dizzy.

He slaps her hard across her right cheek. She stumbles to the side to keep from falling. He grabs her by the shirt and hauls her to her feet, only to shake her until I imagine her teeth rattling. "Fucking bitch. I've told you a thousand times not to talk to me like that."

A flush of anger floods from my core to my limbs and zings through my fingers and toes. I lunge forward and break into a sprint. Wind whips up my hair. Wet strands lash across my face. As I approach full speed, the man turns his head and glances over his shoulder. His face contorts with a mixture of hostility and confusion. "What the fu…"

His sentence trails off as I leap onto his back. My legs wrap around his waist like a vise. One arm wraps around his neck while the other lands blow after blow to his temple. He stumbles around to compensate for my weight, trying to reach around to grab me at the same time. The woman is crying and screaming. Thoughts race through my head faster and faster. Blood pumps through my veins. I know what I'm doing is insane, but I'm already doing it and it doesn't matter. I've crossed a line that I can't go back on. I keep punching over and over again. My hand throbs. Every cell in my body zings.

He manages to reach around and grabs a fistful of my hair. My mind flashes back to all the times Jake pulled my hair, and how it disempowered me. How it angered me. He yanks so hard that tears spring from my eyes and I lose my grip around his waist. I release my legs and scramble to find footing, knowing that he will turn and unleash his wrath. His arm jerks back hard just as my feet hit the ground and I tumble to the asphalt.

I roll to my stomach and crawl as fast as I can to get away. I hear him coming. My knees scrape against asphalt through my pants as I scurry across the pavement toward the object I have my eye on. My right hand wraps around it as his fingers encircle my ankle and drag me toward him.

With a long two-by-four in my grip, I flip to my back and bring the solid piece of wood around in a long, dangerous arc, like a batter swinging his bat for the first game of the season. Just a little shaky, but with a ton of power behind it. He tries to duck back, but the slab of wood connects with his skull before he can get far enough away. The sound is dull and sickening. My stomach quivers, but I leap to my feet while he falls to the ground in slow motion. Dazed, he grabs his head and goes down to one knee. He wobbles, then falls forward face down on the concrete.

"Oh my god, Oh, my god. You killed him." The

woman kneels to his side, her face pale.

I'm trembling. With fear. With adrenaline. With a little bit of excitement. I'm wild. I'm alive.

The man mumbles and groans. He's alive.

I look at the woman, expecting her to cry or scream or threaten me. She glances around nervously. "Hurry, leave. Before someone sees you."

"What?"

Her brows draw together and her lips purse tight. "I said go. When he comes to he'll be angry but he'll be embarrassed too. He won't report this. You're a girl. He'd die first. And he has no idea who you are. So go. I won't say anything. You'll never see me again."

I hesitate. This feels wrong.

Sirens echo in the distance. I know they aren't coming our way, but still, maybe someone heard the commotion and called the police.

The man groans again. She steps forward. "Please. Just go," she begs.

"But what about you?"

"I'll be fine. He won't do anything. Not tonight. Besides, I've been dealing with him a long time. I know how to handle him."

"Well, you shouldn't be."

She nods. The look on her face is resignation. "I know. Now, please go, before he comes to."

Images of police and a jail cell taunt me. Knowing it's my best option, I turn to look for my keys. They lay close to a pile of wood. I snatch them, then turn and run. Around the corner. Down the alley. To my car. All the way home I replay the events over and over again. Adrenaline courses through my body. Parts of my body begin to throb and I know where I'll have bruises in the morning. On the right side of my skull, a deep ache pulses from when he grabbed me by my hair. Fresh rage washes over me. I swerve into a parking spot half a block down from my building. Shove it into park, turn the key. Swing the door open and slide out, slamming it behind me as I bolt up the sidewalk and up my front stairs.

Inside my apartment I march with purpose to my bathroom. Flick on the switch. Ignore the woman in the reflection and dig through my drawers. Shuffling through each one, I grow more agitated and hell bent on my mission. I know they're in here somewhere. My fingers hit metal and hook through the handle of my hair scissors.

Finally facing the woman in the mirror, I lean forward over the sink and start hacking away. Large clumps of curly hair fall away, easing the weight on my soul with every snip of the scissors. I can't seem to cut fast enough. Cut. Cut. Cut. *Get rid of this fucking hair*. I'm breathing so fast I feel close to hyperventilating, dizzy and euphoric. I let out a dark moan that starts deep in my chest. As it rises in my throat, it escalates in pitch and decibels as I decide to let it evolve into a full-fledged scream. My neighbors probably think I'm being murdered or losing my mind. I don't care. It feels good. I scream again and again, watching the way the scissors dance around my scalp, trimming and hacking without reserve. I snip and slice until I have nothing more than an inch and a half all over my head. It's

183

choppy and messy and no one could possibly get a grip on it. No. One. Ever. Again.

I stop and stare at the woman in the mirror and barely recognize her. Her eyes are wild. But I like her so much more than I liked the other woman. This woman isn't afraid. This woman will fight for what she believes in. This woman has fire in her eyes.

I stare at her for another few moments and let my senses settle. Slowly, my muscles relax, the tension oozing from each cell in exquisite release. My breathing returns to a normal pace. Calmness eases in, an unknown sensation.

I slip out of my clothes and hop into the shower, relishing in the way the hot water seems to wash away the woman I used to be. When I'm thoroughly cleansed, I step out, dry off with a large white towel, and crawl into an over-sized t-shirt. I'm calm. I'm not anxious or afraid. I have no desire to cut myself tonight. I feel…sleepy.

I get into bed, turn off the light, and close my eyes, knowing that I'm going to sleep better than I have in months.

***

A bang, bang, banging wakes me from a deep sleep. Face down on my bed, I raise off the pillow and glance toward the clock, smacking my dry lips together. It's nine a.m. I blink and stare longer. There's no way that can be right. I haven't slept through the night in longer than I care to think about. Definitely haven't slept in this long either.

Bang, bang, bang. "I know you're in there, Tessa. I saw your car out front. Open the dang door."

Terin. I roll to my back with a sigh and run my fingers through my hair. A moment of realization passes over me when my fingers brush through my short, choppy cut. Memories of the night before flash before me and I have to stifle a laugh. Feeling lighthearted and oddly happy, I throw back the covers as Terin pounds out another round of persistent knocking. My body is achy and sore, but I still feel better than I have in longer than I can recall.

"I'm coming, I'm coming. Chill your motorboat, woman!"

I shuffle to the door and prepare to face my best friend.

It's fascinating to watch her expression shift so quickly from exasperation to confusion to shock as she takes in my appearance.

"Holy mother of God, woman! What in the hell happened to your hair?"

I reach up with a smirk and run my fingers through it again. Feels nice. "I cut it." I turn and walk away, leaving the door wide open for her to come on in. "I need some coffee. Do you want some?"

The door closes and I hear her right behind me. "Yes, coffee is always good, but not until you tell me what you did to your hair and why? And why in the hell do you still not have a phone? Do you know how much of a pain in the ass it is to come all the way over just to tell you something?"

185

"Not really, but I'm sure you're about to tell me." Suppressing a giggle, I reach up into the cupboard and pull out two coffee cups, then turn to the Keurig, ignoring the sharp pain in my ribcage on the right side.

"Oh, my God! What happened to your knees?"

Startled, I glance down at my bare knees, suddenly aware that I'm still only in my sleeping shirt. My knees are red and angry looking, with gnarly scratches halfway down my shins. Now that I'm aware of them, they sting. Fresh scabs cover areas of broken skin. How do I explain this?

"Oh, hmm, yeah, I uh…"

"Dude, you're freaking me out. What is going on?"

I roll my eyes and return to my chore of making our coffee. "Yes, I'm fine. Just sit down. Let me make some damn coffee, and I'll tell you all about it. Okay?"

An exasperated sigh fills the kitchen. "Okay, fine." The chair screeches against the floor as she pulls it out and plops down. "But I'm not a patient person, so let's go on with it."

Thirty minutes later she sits across the table from me with wide, astonished eyes. "What the hell?"

"What?"

She shakes her head. "I don't even know what to say to you right now. You sit there and tell me about how much you've been suffering all this time. Panic attacks, insomnia, and freaking cutting yourself. And I'm thinking, yeah, I knew you were struggling, but I had no idea how much. What kind of a friend am I? How could I have not known?"

"How would you have known, Terin? I've been hiding it. I've been hiding from everything."

"Yeah, but then out of the blue, you see some woman get attacked and you go all ape shit on her husband. Pretty much beat his ass. Then come home and cut all your gorgeous hair off? I mean, what am I supposed to think? 'Cause to most people it would seem that you may have flipped your freaking lid. I'm wondering if I need to check you into a hospital or something. Yet, you're sitting there all calm and collected and telling me you feel better than you have in years. Bruised and beat all to hell, but cool as a cucumber."

I sip on my coffee, enjoying the strong, bitter flavor. "Better than I ever have in my life, actually."

Terin leans back in her chair and eyeballs me with contemplative, thoughtful eyes. Taking it all in. "So what does all of this mean?"

I shrug. "I don't know."

She chuckles. "Well, one thing is for sure. We're going to the salon today and fixing that train wreck on your head. What kind of a friend would I be if I let you walk around like that?"

I burst into laughter, spitting coffee out of my mouth. She laughs with me. I wipe my chin and laugh harder, tears now spilling down my cheeks. I snort. Our laughter crescendos and melds into one beautiful sound. I feel free.

CHAPTER TWENTY

Terin and I stroll down the busy sidewalks, sipping on our hot mochas. The chocolatey drink is rich and comforting, warming me from the inside out. I resist the urge to run my fingers through my short haircut for the hundredth time. A burst of wind picks up, scattering leaves along our path. The hairs on my neck stand up as the frosty air caresses the back of my neck. I like how it makes me feel weightless, as if the long hair I had all of my life had been weighing me down all of this time, and now it's gone. My neck stretches longer, more elegant. My spine is straighter when I walk, more confident. There's a bounce to my step. I know I'm not the only one who notices either. People watch me more. I catch their eye. In the last twenty-four hours I've become a different person.

I stop short when I see a familiar image staring back at me from an old vintage-clothing store window.

"What?" Terin asks, staring at me with wide eyes.

The image of a phoenix rising from the flames splays over the front of an old worn t-shirt. I shiver as the power of it washes over me. I fight the urge to walk into the store. I want to buy it but I shake my head and keep walking. I haven't earned it. Not yet. "Nothing. It's nothing." I keep walking but the image burns in my mind.

As if trying to read my thoughts, Terin interjects. "So now what?"

I take a slow sip of my coffee, careful not to burn my tongue, then shrug. "What do you mean? Like, what are we going to do now?"

"Well, I guess that too, but I was actually referring to more along the lines of what are you going to do now? You had this huge breakthrough last night, call it a nervous breakdown, or a violent rampage, whatever. The point is, you've had a revelation of sorts and now you're better? I guess I just feel like there's something next. Like this is the beginning of something."

I purse my lips and ponder over Terin's conjecture while we wait to cross the street. One more block until we reach my apartment. "I haven't thought that far ahead yet, I guess. The last twenty-four hours have been a bit of a whirlwind. I've been kind of enjoying it, to be honest. Even the bumps and bruises feel good, in a weird way."

"And you should be! I mean, not the bumps-and-bruises part. That's a little crazy. But you know what I mean. I wasn't trying to rain on your parade. I'm sorry."

I stop walking and put a hand on her shoulder. She stops and looks at me with hesitation.

"It's okay, don't be sorry. I'm not upset. Well, maybe I am, but not because of what you said."

She cocks her head. "Then why?"

I let out a deep sigh. "It made me realize that this feeling, this sense of empowerment and freedom that I'm basking in right now, it might not last. Maybe tonight, when I'm all alone again, the anxiety and terror will creep back in. Maybe I'm just fooling myself today."

Terin shakes her head briskly. "Nope, nope. Don't even go there. That's no way to end this day. You and I have had a great afternoon. You look amazing with your new sassy haircut. I've enjoyed seeing my old friend again, bolder and more beautiful than ever. If you find yourself struggling tonight, then give me a call and I'll be over in a heartbeat. I'll come over with a bottle of wine and we'll have a sleepover. But right now, you're going to enjoy your well-deserved, hard-earned good day! Do you hear me?"

I nod and bite my lip. "Yeah, I hear you." I offer a thin smile, hoping she won't see that I'm forcing it. I can't stand the idea of losing this feeling.

Her brows furrow. I know she sees my inner struggle. "Hey, listen, here's what you're going to do. You're going to think about what you can do to keep this newfound positivity and confidence. You're going to think of ways to continue to build on what you started. Whether it's your self-defense class, the support group, it doesn't matter. You're going to find what makes you feel strong and you're going to do that. Make sense?"

Her words echo in my mind and the gears start

clinking and chugging along as new thoughts are born. Before I can string them together into a linear and coherent pattern, she tugs at my coat.

"Come on, let's get inside. I'm freezing out here."

I tuck these fresh, underdeveloped concepts into the back of my mind so I can take them out and dissect them later tonight. I shuffle after Terin to keep up.

"By the way, I asked about your phone earlier but shit got weird, so we never really discussed it. Are you ever going to try to get your phone back from Tom or what?"

We come to the front stair of the apartment. I reach into my pocket and pull out the key. "I've thought about it a few hundred thousand times but that's as far as I got. He swears he doesn't have it but I know I left it in his car."

She follows close behind, eager to get into the warm building. "Well, I can go over there if you want. Just give me his address."

Memories of the one time I was ever at Tom's home, unannounced and unwelcome, come flooding forward. I cringe on the inside, shame overwhelming me all over again. "No, that's not necessary. I think I'll just go buy a new phone. That one was almost two years old anyway. Time for an upgrade. To be honest, I enjoyed not having a phone for a while, but I know you're right. I need to get one again."

Entering my unit, we shrug out of our jackets and toss them to the couch rather than taking the time to hang them. Terin plops down in the rocking chair by the window. Her favorite spot. Within seconds she's rocking back and forth with her typical enthusiasm.

"Okay, fine. So you'll get a new phone. But that still doesn't explain why he's denying he has it. Why not just give it back? You'd think by now, nearly two months later, he'd have dropped by or put it in the mail or something. I mean, come on. It's common courtesy. Have you even heard from the rat bastard?"

This conversation has me on edge. Memories of the day Tom stopped by to see me in the hospital flood back. He seemed so odd that day. So out of sorts, like he was nervous. Then again, I was drugged and still disoriented from my whole ordeal. That entire week blurs together now, like a bad dream pieced together. The good feelings from earlier today are gone. "You know, maybe he's telling the truth and he really doesn't have it. I mean, just because I thought it must have fallen out in his car that night doesn't mean that it did. Maybe I lost it somewhere between there and when I was grabbed."

"Hmm, maybe…I'm just not sure. I think we should go over there and at least ask Tom about it."

I march to the kitchen. "I'm hungry. Are you hungry? Do you want something to eat? Maybe some chips and salsa?"

"Okay, so we're changing the subject. Fine. But that's not the last of it, missy."

"I know." I turn my focus to making a plate of cold cuts with cheese and crackers along with chips and salsa, as promised. We talk nonchalantly about the weather and her new boots and the latest season of *Dancing With The Stars*. Quietly, methodically, I contemplate over the things she and I have discussed today. Answers to her questions play out in my mind. I know what must be done. I can't, I won't, tell her, but my heart beats faster in anticipation. I can't wait.

***

As soon as Terin leaves, I dart to the living room window to gauge my timing. It's already four thirty in the afternoon, so there's only about another forty-minutes before the remaining daylight is completely swallowed up by winter's darkness. With it being a Friday night, there will be plenty of nightlife activities around the city. If I hurry, I should be able to be out and about by nine or ten.

That's when things start getting good, anyway.

I dash down the hallway and into my bedroom. Rifling through my drawers and closets, I toss everything that I think I might be able to use to my bed. Within minutes I'm damp with a thin layer of sweat and a little frustrated. I don't have exactly what I want for tonight's excursion, but I'll have to make do. Tomorrow I'll have to do some shopping.

For now, I forage through the pile of clothing that I've gathered and piece together my outfit for the evening. I'm even sweatier by the time I try on six different combinations and finally settle on what I think will at least get the job done. I don't really even have a plan. Just an amorphous need to go out into the world and seek out that which I'm craving.

An itch that needs scratched.

I stand in front of the full-length mirror on the wall by the bathroom door. Dressed in black from head to toe, the matching workout wear is form-fitting, comfortable, and made of thin material that is easy to move in. Breathable. Innocuous. I slip into my black sneakers and grimace because I wish the pink Nike swoosh symbol wasn't there. Not a big deal. Something is missing, though. I return to the closet in search of my stash of hats and pull out an old snap-back of my dad's. I'd worn it years ago when I was helping him bring in firewood and never gave it back. At thirteen, I'd known he and my mom were having a lot of marital problems and knew they would someday split. Looking back, I think I must have wanted to keep a piece of him just in case they did break up. It took another decade and a whole lot of heartache for them to actually go their separate ways, but now I hold the hat in my hands, looking at the woman facing me in the mirror, and feel gratitude. I know my dad shouldn't have cheated on my mom, but I also know that he fought depression from living with her passive-aggressive condescending insults for a lot longer.

Though it was never outright acknowledged, I know they married before they turned eighteen because I was on the way. They both made the best of a sticky situation before they even knew who they really were in this world, much less what they wanted.

We don't always get to choose who we want to be initially. But it seems, if we're lucky, we eventually get the opportunity to choose who we

194

want to be in the end. With that thought in mind, I put the hat on and pull the bill down so that it fits secure over my short hair. I look like I'm simply a woman ready to go for a jog. No big deal.

I head to the kitchen and pluck my favorite knife from the cutting block. The one I've been fond of lately as I've carved out my unyielding anger into my flesh. Then I dig through my sewing materials and find a strong piece of elastic. It takes me over an hour, but eventually I'm happy with the strap I've made to hold the knife around my calf. I slip it on, then sheath the knife into place. I pull the thin fabric of my pants down, and though you can make out an object there, it's obscure and not that noticeable. I jump up and down to ensure it's secure. I'm quite pleased with myself. It's not bad for a quick-fix solution. Tomorrow I'll find something better.

Unsure of how or what I'm searching for this evening, I leave my apartment sure of only one thing. Anxiety and fear will not claim me again tonight. Or ever again.

CHAPTER TWENTY-ONE

I've been walking the streets for hours. My feet hurt. My back aches. I'm a little hungry. But mostly I'm hugely disappointed. Though it's well past eleven, nothing is going on. Nothing interesting, anyway. The streets are crowded with people bustling about from place to place in search of exciting shenanigans. Drunken debauchery of all sorts can be found on every corner, but so far nothing more harmful than the usual from your typical sloppy drunks, rowdy boys and girls looking to get laid, and the occasional yelling match in the street before a friend breaks it up and the fun dissipates too quickly. Very lame.

It's not fair. I'd anticipated a bit more excitement for the evening. Instead, I've wandered the streets in search of something I can't quite name.

Giving in to my growling stomach, I opt to go into a small pizzeria on the corner where I've been loitering the last half hour. The inviting smells of pizza dough and spices welcome me in. It's warm and dry inside and I'm glad I wandered in because I'm suddenly ravenous, practically drooling.

I sidle up to the counter to order a slice of meat-lover's pizza and a Coke. I take my meal and look for an open place to sit. For being so late, the place is fairly full. There's an empty spot in the corner, by an elderly man who looks like he's seen the better side of hell over the course of his life. His skin is pocked and marred. A scar runs up his entire right arm, which is still lean and muscular given his age. Tattoos garnish a majority of his exposed skin, including his neck. A brief moment of hesitation washes over me before I squash it away.

As I approach, I notice his hands tremble as he eats a piece of pizza. He glances my way and I recognize that glassy, inebriated stare. He's been drinking for...well, for a long damn time. I offer a brief smile and pass by. When he smiles back, I notice that he's missing a fair amount of teeth. Sadness encompasses me as I wonder what this man has been through in his life. War? Battles? Violence. Heartache. Addiction. Loss. All of the above. My appetite wanes. I make my way to my seat, frustrated with life. Why does it have to be so hard? Why all the suffering? Why so many battles? I keep my head down and slowly eat my pizza, enjoying it much less than I had intended. The evening as a whole has not gone as I intended. Then again, it rarely does.

Feeling defeated and deflated, I gather my trash. As I pass the man on my way out, I can't help but notice his food is gone but he still sits there, his head slightly hung. Is he homeless? Is this the warmest spot to hang out for as long as possible before he goes back out into the cold? I reach into my jacket pocket and pull out a ten-dollar bill, quickly placing it on the table next to his hand and walking away before he can say anything.

When I walk out the front door, the cold air smacks me in the face and jolts me out of my sad reverie. Now I'm just deflated. Back to the apartment I go.

Two blocks from my building, I spot a car on the opposite side of the street. The parking lights cut through the dark and a thin film of exhaust escaping the tailpipe indicates the car is running. Probably someone dropping off a date. Keeping my steady stride, my mind toys with a myriad of possibilities as I imagine what the date would have been like. A first date? Did it go well? Are they kissing goodnight?

A door up ahead on my left slams. Attention diverted, I follow the sound to see a woman clambering down the steps of an older brick building. Even from this distance I recognize her disheveled state. Her hair spills out of a messy topknot on her head. Her short skirt inches further up her thin thighs as she scurries down the steps. She wears a sequined tank top, one strap haphazardly hanging off her shoulder. She carries her high heels in one hand, too hurried to put them on. I recognize her. She's the prostitute who had frequented my street a few months back. I haven't seen her in a couple of weeks.

As she hits the sidewalk, she's already glancing

up and down the street before she crosses, and I can tell she's heading toward the parked car across the road. The window rolls down and a man leans out. "What the hell took you so damn long?" he barks. I note a slight Hispanic accent.

My pace slows and I decide to hang back, keep my distance.

She waits for a car to pass before she pads barefoot across the street. "I'm sorry, Stone. I'm sorry. Don't be angry, it's not my fault."

The driver's-side door swings open and the man called Stone steps out. He appears shockingly short, not much taller than the car. But his upper body is stocky, like he never skips a day at the gym.

"Don't give me that shit, Kim. You're late every damn time. Get your ass over here."

She approaches the car and hesitates before closing the last four feet. She reaches into the top of her shirt and pulls out a wad of bills from her bra. "Here's the money. I made extra. He wanted extra. That's why I'm late. Isn't that great?"

The desperation in her trembling voice triggers anxiety and anger within me. I sense how this will end.

In one swift move, he steps forward and snatches her by the front of her shirt. "No, it's not fucking great. You don't get to make those decisions. I do."

My teeth hurt from clenching so hard, but I know I can't make an irrational move that would surely end badly for her. I have to be patient, so I hang back in the shadows, away from the light of the streetlamps. I want to help this woman. I came out looking for something like this. Now that it's

199

staring me in the face, I have no idea how to handle it.

Think. Be smarter.

The sound of his palm smacking her across the face snaps me out of it. I have to do something. Like a runner waiting for the start gun to go off, I clench my fists and crouch low, reaching for my knife. My palms sweat, so I make sure to grip it tightly while waiting for the right moment. I look up and down the street. No one is around. Thin clouds drift over the half moon. A baby cries in the distance. The woman sobs quietly as the man named Stone shoves her into the car through the driver's-side door.

With his back to me, I charge into a full sprint. I'm light on my feet, but my heart thunders in time with every step I take. Flashes of Vance and Jake rush forward, blinding me to any remaining rational thought. Seconds before I'm within arm's reach, I see Kim just over his shoulder as she scoots into the passenger seat and looks up. Her eyes widen and her mouth forms an O shape as I lunge forward. Startled by her expression, he spins on his heel. But my blade slips into his flank before he makes it around.

He grunts. Hot liquid spills over my fist. A wave of nausea washes over me. What have I done? As his legs buckle beneath him, he falls to one knee. He twists his head up and stares into my face with pain and shock and confusion. Kim screams out in a high-pitched frenzy.

Look at her. Look at him. What have I done? The weight of it all comes crashing over me.

His brows furrow, and sweat slicks over his face in the moonlight. Anger replaces confusion and he lashes out with his left hand to grab my legs. I leap back and he misses, falling forward with another grunt of pain. The knife sticks out of his left kidney area ominously. I've made a grave mistake. I step forward and yank the knife from his body. He yells and flings his arm to the side, trying to hit me. I take three shaky steps back before I turn and run as fast as my legs will take me.

***

What have I done? What have I done? Breathe in. Breathe out. Oh fuck!

Scrubbing blood from my hands in the bathroom sink, I feel like I might pass out. My lips and hands buzz and I realize I'm hyperventilating. *Breathe. Oh fuck!* Have I lost my mind? What was I thinking? I just stabbed a man. He saw my face. He's going to find me and kill me. If I'm not arrested and thrown into jail for attempted murder first.

I look up at the woman staring back at me. Her lips are white. Her jaw trembles with fear. I have lost my mind. I rip the hat off my head and run a wet hand through my short hair. What am I going to do? I turn off the water and strip out of my clothes. Shower. Then get rid of the knife. My hands shake violently as I scrub from head to toe, making sure to take at least the first layer of skin off.

The scalding hot water does very little to heat my frigid bones. I can't stop shaking. Hop out of the shower. Dry off with a few rigid strokes from head

201

to toe. I'm dizzy. I need to lie down. I wrap the towel around my body and cinch it tight against my breasts before padding down the hall to the bedroom. I crawl onto the bed and lie on my back to stare at the ceiling. Hours pass. My mind devours itself with guilt and shame and fear. Then it slowly begins to settle. I've crossed a line. My breathing slows with the acceptance of the crime I've just committed.

A calm knowing oozes in and pushes out the fear. I know what must be done.

As the first light of day creeps into the horizon of the dark sky, I quietly slip into jeans and a sweatshirt, then pull on a different pair of shoes. In the bathroom I get on my hands and knees and dig through a box under the bathroom sink. I'm positive I still have supplies from back when my mom's diabetes had been out of control and I'd had to administer her shots. I bump my head on the counter and swear under my breath before finally pulling the box out. Dust covers a few medical supplies that I've collected over the years for various reasons. Gauze, tape, a wrist splint, rubbing alcohol, syringes. And six remaining vials of insulin. Not sure why I've kept them all these years. I check the dates. They are not only expired, but they require refrigeration. But safety isn't my goal here. I just need them to carry their potency. No longer fearful or ashamed, my hand is steady as I draw up every drop.

I leave the apartment and drive to the nearest hospital. On the way, I make a call to the operator.

"St. Francis Hospital admissions, how can I help

you?"

"Yes, this is Officer Sharon Gerald with the Everett Police Department. We had a report come in about a stabbing down on West Boulevard Drive late last night. I'm trying to locate the victim so we can confirm the claim and ask him questions in regards to the matter. Do you mind telling me if you had a man who fits that description come into the emergency room? I'm told his first name is Stone, if that helps."

"No problem at all, Officer. Give me just one moment and I'll look through our database of recent admissions."

A pause fills the line. I hold my breath.

"Let's see here, it looks like we did have a stabbing victim come in last night, but I have him under a different name. He's no longer in the ER. He was transferred to the fourth floor."

"May I have his name?"

"Yes, ma'am, but I can't give it to you over the phone. I'll have to see your identification first before I can give you any further information. Patient privacy and all that."

"Sure. I understand. I'll be in within the next half hour." I hang up and toss the phone to the console between the front seats. Ten minutes later, I wander into the quiet hallways of the hospital, hoping not to be noticed by staff or security. At five in the morning, only the sparse night crew loiters in their nursing stations, tired and waiting patiently for their shift to end. The weight of what I'm about to do stifles every breath, every step I take. *Stop now. Don't do it. Turn around and go home.* But I can't.

When I find his room on the fourth floor, he lies in the bed, asleep and alone. No one sits at his bedside. I imagine a man like this has no real friends. I steal a quick glance left then right before slowly pushing the heavy door open and slipping into the room. An oxygen cannula sits under his nose. Monitors at his bedside record every heartbeat and breath taken. I creep to his bed and look down at this man. He seems less menacing now, his lids soft and closed. His mouth settled into a flat line rather than aggression. I hold my breath and my heart races faster.

I can't do this. I'm not a murderer. I'm not violent at all. I don't even know who I am anymore.

His eyes flutter open and he stares at me with wide, knowing eyes, as if he'd been expecting me. My muscles spasm, then freeze. We hold gazes, sealed in this one fateful moment of indecision.

The corners of his mouth slowly turn upward, revealing one gold incisor tooth among a mouthful of surprisingly white teeth. "I know you. I've seen you around the neighborhood. I know where you live."

I shake my head. "No." My words come out in a breathless whisper.

His brows raise. "Oh, yes I do. I know most things about my neighborhoods. I make it my business to know. You think I'm stupid?"

I shake my head again. "No."

He laughs, then winces in pain. "Dammit."

I think of turning and running out of the room, but then what? I'm stuck. I have no idea what I should do.

He squints, glowering through his thick lashes. "I'm glad you came. I thought you might. What did you think you would do once you got here? Take another stab at me? You gonna kill me?"

My lips part but I remain silent. Only my breathing fills the gap of silence in the room.

He chuckles. Shivers tingle up my spine.

"Of course you won't. It's not in you. You're trying to be someone you're not. I've seen it a hundred times. But you done messed with the wrong person and got in over your head. Just wait until I get out of here, bitch. I'm going to kill you, slowly and painfully. But first, I'm going to let you watch me kill the girl you were trying to protect. How's that for irony?"

A metallic taste fills my mouth and I realize I've been biting my cheeks. Rage fills every cell. Yet, I feel calm. A decision has been made. I step forward, reach out, and grab his IV tubing. He tries to sit up, but grunts in pain. He flails his arms, but with a few deft movements, I pull the needle out of my pocket, uncap it, and quickly inject the deadly dose of insulin into the line.

His eyes widen. "What the fuck did you do?"

I lean over him and cover his mouth with both of my hands, one knee propped on the edge of the bed. He moans and squirms but he is weak from the loss of blood, so I press harder against his mouth, leaning in with all of my weight, and look into his eyes as his body starts to shake and seizure, the medicine hitting his system like snake venom. I meet his gaze with peace. "I did what had to be done," I whisper as his lids flutter and his eyes roll

205

back.

When it's over, I step back. "Good night." I turn and walk out the door, pulling my hood over my head as I sneak out. No one notices as an insignificant woman leaves the building while an evil man lies in bed and dies from an insulin overdose.

CHAPTER TWENTY-TWO

His leg sweeps out, but I see the move from the corner of my eye. I leap sideways to avoid the impact, then leap back and grab him from behind as he finishes his spin. At the peak of my jump, I wrap my right bicep around his neck and lock my left hand around to secure the grip, then squeeze.

Next thing I know, I'm on my back with a thud. Air whooshes from my lungs in a violent exhale. I release my grip and gasp for air. The weight of his body shifts as he grunts and rolls away.

"That was actually really good up until the end there, Tess. Next time, though, keep your grip, even if you end up on your back."

Holding my chest and catching my breath, I offer Tobin a sideways glare. "I'll be sure to remember that next time."

One side of his mouth turns up in a sideways grin. "Don't be a poor sport. You know I'm right. If you had just held on, you would have had the upper hand. You had me in a vise grip, and if you had pushed through, I would have passed out already."

I roll my eyes dramatically then sit up and pop up to my feet. "Then let's do it again."

He laughs. "That a girl." He pauses, his head cocked to the side, as if sizing me up. "Something's changed in you lately. And I'm not just talking about your hair, which I like, by the way. It's...it looks pretty on you. But it's more than that, you seem...better."

That takes me off guard, so I straighten my back and self-consciously run a hand through my hair. "Yeah, well, compared to what?" When he doesn't answer, I shrug. "I guess I feel a bit better lately."

"I can see it in the way you move. You're more confident. More aggressive. That shy timidity seems to have faded away. I only see it here and there for a moment and then it's gone."

I nod and ponder his statement. "Good."

"Do you think it's our lessons?"

I fight the urge to laugh out loud. "Yeah, that's it." If he only knew.

He frowns, but I find his boyish pout cuter than I'd like.

"Well, what is it then? Come on, tell me your secret."

The word *secret* punches me in the stomach. The way that pimp lay in his hospital bed dying a karmic death enters my mind. It takes everything I have to keep my facial expression from revealing my sudden change of mood.

His voice deepens and softens. "You're a mystery to me."

My body reacts to the slight lilt of seduction in his tone. I don't want to feel like this toward Tobin. Or anyone, for that matter. Ignoring his statement, I bend at the knees and prepare for another round of sparring. "Come on, let's go again."

We are silent for the remainder of my lesson, the tension building between us, threatening to take our friendship to uncharted territory. Later, washed up and famished, I head out the back door of the gym.

"Hold on, wait for me."

With my right foot jammed in the door, I turn to see Tobin jogging toward me, his gym bag bouncing lightly over his shoulder.

He slows to a walk as he nears. "I was wondering if you wanted to get something to eat down the street. I'm starving."

My stomach growls at the mere mention of food. "Food?"

"Yeah, food, like something to eat."

I giggle nervously. "I don't know. I was just going to head home."

"Oh, come on, it's just some food. You're hungry. I'm hungry. Let's get something to eat. I promise I won't bite. There's nothing to be scared of with me."

"I'm not scared."

He stares me down and waits for my next move. Daring me to prove him wrong.

I shrug. "Okay, fine. Just something quick."

He breaks into a huge grin, showing that one small dimple on the left cheek, and I find myself unable to keep from smiling back. I acquiesce and we walk side by side in silence to a small pub down the street that specializes in local microbrews and fish-and-chips.

Once we're settled, he grabs one of the menus off the table and flips through.

I eye him carefully over the top of mine. "So, what's this really about? I can tell you want to talk about something. You didn't just want to take me out for a quick bite to eat." It still surprises me that I can be this forthright now. A few months ago I would have died of humiliation just from the thought of being so bold.

He sighs and lays the menu flat. "Well, that's not entirely true. I did want to take you out. In fact I'd prefer to take you somewhere nicer and make more of a deal of it, but I know you're not ready for that yet."

I blink and keep a straight face, reaching for one of the iced waters on the table.

"Did you hear about the stabbing in your neighborhood the other night?"

Slowly, I sip from the glass, cool water wets my suddenly dry mouth. I make sure to keep eye contact. I set the glass down and wipe condensation from the tips of my fingers onto the napkin to my right side. Time slows down. "I heard some of my neighbors mumbling about it this morning but I didn't catch the details."

The waiter approaches. "Are you ready to order? Can I start you off with something other than water to drink?"

"I'll have an iced tea and a Caesar salad." I sit back against the booth and wait for Tobin to give his order.

When the waiter leaves, he props his elbows on the table and leans forward a bit, showing me that I have his full attention. "So back to what we were discussing, no one mentioned seeing the guy who did it? No one witnessed the incident?"

"Why do you automatically assume it was a man?"

It's his turn to look surprised. His left eye squints as he processes the question. "Well, other than the prostitute who took him to the hospital, no one saw the crime, as far as I've heard, and the man who was stabbed wouldn't say who did it. She's not talking either. I guess I just assumed it was a man, based on experience with other crimes such as this. Now he's dead, so we won't be able to get further details from him, obviously."

"He died, huh?"

"Yeah. At the hospital. Kind of odd that neither he nor the woman would say anything about who attacked him. I can't decide if it's because he was protecting someone or just biding his time until he could seek revenge on his own. It's fairly typical for people associated with that arena of crime to think like that. You know, keep the cops out of it no matter what. Kind of a gang mentality. We're the enemy and they'll take care of business the way they see fit." He leans back in the booth and crosses his arms over his chest. I can't help but notice the way his t-shirt fits snug over his broad shoulders and toned biceps. Why am I thinking of this as we discuss the very crime I committed?

"So, what all did you hear from your neighbors then?"

211

"Are you asking me as a cop or as a civilian?"

He cocks his head to the side. "Both. I'm not on the case, but a few of my fellow officers are and we need more information on who could have been the perp. But also, it was close to where you live and I'm worried about you. I don't want you walking around at night alone until we catch this guy."

He's worried about me. I'm not sure how to feel about that. "Well, like I said before, I didn't hear details. I didn't want to. However, one of the women in the building did mention that the victim was a pimp and a drug dealer that's been wreaking havoc around here for quite some time. Sounded like a pretty nasty individual to me, so maybe your perp did everyone a favor."

"I can't argue that, but a crime's a crime, and it's our job to get to the bottom of these things. Murder is murder, no matter which way you dice it."

Murder. I swallow around the lump in my throat and nod, afraid to respond.

I'm grateful when he changes the subject to more innocuous topics such as the weather and the self-defense class. I do my best to engage, but the word *murder* floats around in my brain like a wispy bit of fog that refuses to clear.

Later, when he walks me back to my car parked in front of the gym, it's completely dark out. Night has fallen, but the weather is oddly mild for the time of year. I sense the tension building between us again and I know he's about to make a move before he actually does. Just as we approach my car, I step ahead, but his hand slips into mine and pulls me around so that I'm facing him. My heart races but

I'm not afraid. I'm not fighting it. I'm just going to let it happen.

His palm is warm and I like the way it envelopes mine. I tilt my chin up. Watching. Waiting. His eyes search mine. He's giving me that extra moment to pull away. I wait patiently. Anticipating the next few moments.

He reaches up with the other hand and gently runs his fingers through the short hair at the nape of my neck. A shiver runs down my spine. My stomach quivers.

He moves his hand down my neck and along my jaw until his thumb caresses my cheek. This touch is so gentle, so inviting. Unlike anything I've ever experienced. I want to lean into it and purr from enjoyment, but I hold very still and allow it to happen ever so slowly, almost painfully. I've felt a lot of new feelings lately. I want to cherish this one.

My lips part slightly as he leans in. *Breathe in, breathe out.* He smells delicious. I close my eyes moments before his lips graze mine. It's a soft touch, barely there. I open my mouth and invite him in. A growl rumbles in his chest and he pulls me against his body, drinking me in. My arms slide up around his neck, while my body presses into his warmth. His hands are in my hair, then cupping my face. We are hungry for each other and it's so much more than I would have anticipated.

When he pulls away I feel lost. I stare up at him, wanting more. He holds my face in both hands and gazes down at me as if he's as surprised and lost as I am. "Are you okay?"

I blink. "Yeah, I'm okay. That's a weird question

to ask right now."

He chuckles softly. "I just don't want to frighten you off. You've been through a lot, and you're so hard to read. I just don't know where you stand most of the time. Like I said before, you're a mystery to me."

I stretch up on my tiptoes and pull him down so I can lay another soft kiss on his lips. Very quick, very gentle, then pull away. "I'm fine. It was nice. But I'm going to go home now." I step back and let his arms fall away. A sudden sense of loneliness fills my core and I realize that I crave his presence. Which is why I must go home now.

I dig my keys out of my pocket as I turn toward the car. Hit the unlock button and open the door. Turn and offer a nonchalant smile. He stands with his arms dropped to his side, a baffled expression haunting his features.

"I'll see you in class tomorrow."

He nods. "Okay. See you tomorrow. Can I call you later?"

I shake my head. "Still don't have a phone. I promised my best friend I'd get a new one this weekend." Without another word I slip into the driver's seat and start the car. I don't look back as I drive away. Who was that woman back there kissing Tobin? Who is that woman who killed a man as he lay in a hospital bed?

Who is this woman I'm becoming? She intrigues me. She frightens me.

Later in the evening, I lie awake in bed replaying our kiss on a city street in Everett. Not the most romantic of places, but it didn't detract from the way he swept me away in that brief moment. A smile tugs at the corners of my mouth and I suddenly wish I had my cell phone so he could have called tonight like he wanted.

The thought of my cell phone piques my interest. I sit upright in bed and swing my legs over the edge, processing an idea. I stand and pad over to where my laptop sits on my dresser by the window. Standing in the dark, I open it and wait for the screen to come alive, then type in my password. I don't know why I never thought of this before. I log into my Verizon account and scroll through my settings. There it is. The tracker. I'd forgotten that I'd had the feature activated. I should be able to see exactly where my phone is, even if it's dead.

I click on the link and wait for it to load. With another couple of clicks, I'm on the page where it loads the map. A red dot sits in the center of the screen. A wave of dizziness passes over me. I know that part of town. It's where Tom lives. Why in the hell did he lie and say he didn't have it?

I close the laptop and walk to my bed. I don't know what this means, but I need to decide what I'm going to do about it. Go get my phone or forget about it and move on?

***

The next day, on my way to class, I'm more eager than usual to see Tobin. I want to see how he will react to me since our kiss. I anticipate how it will feel when we spar now during training. It makes my skin tingle. I feel alive again.

215

Because traffic is a nightmare so close to the Christmas holiday, parking is worse, so I park a block and a half away from the gym. The sky is dark, but so far there is no sign of rain. It's only a matter of time, so I quickly gather my things and reach for the handle. Just before I open the door, I spot Tobin another half a block down. He's descending the concrete steps of a restaurant and lounge. I grin with excitement. Another man steps out right behind Tobin.

Tom.

Tobin turns with a grin and shakes Tom's hand. Mortified, I hunch down in my seat and hope that I'm not seen. What are they doing together? Tobin promised he wouldn't talk with Tom. I feel the blood drain from my face. I should have never trusted him. Trust no one. Seems like I would have learned that lesson by now.

Filled with dread and disappointment, I start the car. My hands white knuckle the steering wheel as I glance over my shoulder before pulling into traffic. *NO*. I whip my head forward and slam the car into park again. *No. I'm not doing this.* I'm not running away. I'm fucking sick of running. Instead, I wait and watch.

My pulse throbs through my fingers, reminding me to loosen my grip on the steering wheel. I take in a deep breath, watching Tom's cocky stride saunter down the sidewalk to his car. *Hold the breath. Hold it. Breathe.*

Tobin stands at the curb watching Tom's departure, as well. His body language is stiff, as if he's uncomfortable. Maybe it's the chill in the air today. Maybe it's the deception. My heart races faster as anger mixes with shock over the situation. Take in another deep breath. Gaze shifts toward Tom. He slides into the driver's seat. *Hold the breath*. He pulls away. Switch to Tobin. He's turning away and walking my direction. Knowing I need to act, I swing open my door and step out. Less than half a block away, Tobin glances up as I round the front of the car. Our gazes lock. He stutter steps. I paste a smile onto my wind-stricken face and march forward. I need him to believe that I haven't seen a thing.

His expression is stern, his features strong against the bitter cold. But I know it's a response to seeing me here, now, rather than to the weather.

I wave. "Tobin! Hi. What are you doing here?"

He gives a thin, practiced smile. "Hey, Tess. I'm just on my way to class, of course. Though it's early yet. I should ask you the same thing."

We're face to face now. He stares down at me and a puff of air escapes his lips, proving it's much too cold out today. I shrug. "Eh, just wanted to put in a little extra time at the gym before class started. That okay?"

He nods and glances over his shoulder nervously, as if making sure Tom's nowhere in sight. I've been wracking my brain in the last few moments on how to handle this precarious situation. "Well, I'm glad I ran into you because I have something I want to show you. Can I borrow your cell phone?" He pauses, offering a suspicious sideways glance.

"Uh, sure." He reaches into his back jeans

pocket, types in the passcode, and hands it over. "What's this all about?"

I start dialing, not even sure what I'm doing with this half thought out idea, but sure I'm about to prove to Tobin that Tom is a jerk and a liar. I can't wait to see the look on his face when he finds out his friend has my phone. "Well, I got to thinking about how you said I should get a new phone and then it suddenly dawned on me. Why don't I just call it? Maybe someone found it and will answer?" Knowing no one will answer because the phone is dead at Tom's house, I stare up into his face with a look of guile forcefully plastered to my face, and hold it to my ear waiting for it to ring. After my call attempt I'll log into my account and show him the tracker, as if seeing it for the first time. Then he'll see that Tom has it. "Let's give it a shot." My hands tremble. I'm just flying by the seat of my pants.

"Tess, no!" He reaches for me, but I sidestep and twist my body away and out of his reach.

My lips part in eager anticipation as the first ring echoes in my ear. Before the first ring ends, another ring coincides, matching the sound in an eerie echo. But this ring is close, and in real time. I falter, saliva pooling in the sides of my cheeks as my mind wraps around the two mirroring sounds. Tobin's skin color pales to a yellow pallor. Another ring clangs in my ear, followed by its shadow ring. I glance down, following the trail of sound. Tobin closes his eyes and reaches into his pocket. My arm drops to my side. He holds up my phone. It rings again, louder now that it's out in the open. Singing its truth song.

"My phone." The words fall out in a breathless

gasp.

"It's not what you think."

It feels as if time has slowed to an unmanageable pace. It's thick and dreamy. I'm drowning. "Then what is it? Because it looks like you have my phone."

He sighs. "Yes, it's your phone…"

"I saw you. Just now. I saw you with Tom. You lied. You said you wouldn't talk with him." My words tumble out in a frenzy, one run-on sentence.

His jaw twitches. "I know that's what I said. And I meant it when I said it, but…"

"But what? You decided you didn't mean it after all?"

"I decided that you only asked because you were scared, and as an investigator who takes his job and protecting you very seriously, I knew I had to do what was right, which was retrieve your phone. He met me today and handed it over without a problem. He was more than willing to hand it over. And as promised, I limited my questioning."

"As promised? No. That's not at all what was promised. You said you wouldn't talk to him at all about us. You never said anything about questioning him and it being okay as long as it was, quote unquote *limited*. And you sure as hell didn't say anything about retrieving my phone and not telling me about it."

He rolls his eyes. "I didn't have the chance. I was going to give it to you before class. I wanted to surprise you. That's why I was early."

"Surprise me? Well, good job. I'm surprised. You and my ex-lover just met in a pub and swapped

219

stories."

He shakes his head. "No, that's not what happened. Yesterday I called him. Told him I happened to be the detective on the case and through questioning of witnesses to your case that night, found out that you and he had left the club together. At that point, I asked if he knew where your phone was and he willingly gave it up. No fuss, no muss. It really wasn't a big deal." He steps forward and takes my hand. "I wasn't trying to deceive you, Tessa. You're important to me. I...I care about you."

A whirlwind of toxic thoughts swirl through my mind. Is Tobin really just trying to do something kind for me, a romantic gesture? Is Tom really so innocent that he'd give up my phone so easily? Then why did he keep it for so long? Was he just trying to maintain anonymity in the case? Was he afraid? Confusion fogs my brain and I find myself staring up at Tobin, speechless. His admission of feelings only confuses the matter further.

I take two steps back. My hand leaving his. He takes one forward. I shake my head. "I can't do this right now." I spin on the ball of my left foot and run toward my car. Cold wind assaults the skin on my face. Tobin calls out after me but I know he's not following by the way the sound falls away as distance grows between us. He knows better. I need to be alone right now.

***

I sit straight up in bed, the hairs on my arms

standing up. I'm not sure what startled me. A dream, a sound? All I know is that I'm suddenly wide awake with the stench of fear strong in my nostrils. My back is sweaty and my heart races in my eardrums. I sit quietly, straining to hear any sounds that don't belong.

A stifled bump reaches my ears but it sounds like any other bump in the night in city apartment life. I'm okay. *Breathe.* There's nothing to fear. Tears well up. It frustrates me how easily I become frightened even after my recent transformation. I worry the fear will never really leave. The memory of earlier today flashes into the forefront of my mind. Tobin. Tom. My phone. I'm dreaming. Paranoid.

Another sound floats over the air. This time it's more of a shuffle. A shiver runs down my spine. Maybe I'm not hearing things. I slowly pull back the covers and swing both feet over the side of the bed. I'm careful to set my weight down slowly, so as to not make any sound. Holding my breath, I tiptoe in my own bedroom to the door. I wait and listen, my ear perched next to the small gap between the door and the wall, where it's open a few inches.

Movement catches my eye. I peer and look closer. Down the hall, I can see half of the living room. In the corner, I see a tall figure hovering. Someone is in my home. My mouth goes dry and I pull back before whoever it is sees me. My chest is tight and I fear they will hear my breathing. I have no idea what to do. I have no phone. How stupid of me to have left it behind before running off. Stupid girl. No way to call for help other than screaming but I don't want to bring attention to myself.

What is this man doing in my home? Rage fills my chest as a sense of violation visits me, overriding the terror. I've killed men. I will not allow fear to enter my home. I turn to my closet and reach for the one thing I know will be my best bet for a weapon. Power surges through me as my hand clasps around one of the bedposts of my four poster bed. Quickly, I unscrew it from the frame, then turn, clasping it like a sword.

Every step is cautious, every sensation alive and heightened in my feet and legs as I move to the door. I cringe when the door makes a small but noticeable creak. A scuffle follows. Then footsteps. A blurred image rushes to the front door.

I lunge down the hall, yielding my weapon, determined not to let him get away. He knocks over the table in the foyer, then bolts out the front door. I leap over the hurdle, but my foot catches the edge as I misjudge its height in the dark and stumble to the ground. Swearing under my breath, I scramble to my feet and out the door. I see only the back of the man just as he darts out of the building. But I recognize him immediately.

I know that hair, that jacket.

Goddamn Gerald.

***

An hour later, Tobin sits at my kitchen table while I sip on hot tea. His body language and demeanor have been nothing but professional, and even a bit closed off since I ran to the neighbors and

222

called him to report the break in. Despite his betrayal, he was the first person I thought to call. Even though I'm not sure I can trust him now, I still know what to expect with him. I know he'll do his damn job.

Other police officers mill around the apartment, gathering fingerprints and any other evidence they can find.

"We arrested him based on your description," Tobin says. "It won't take long to match his prints and confirm it was for sure him here tonight."

The tea scalds the tip of my tongue as I take another sip. I welcome it. I'm cold to the bone. "It was him. I'm sure of it."

Tobin's demeanor has been purely professional throughout the process but I sense his underlying concern for my well-being. "Has he ever done anything like this before? Come over unannounced or done anything suspicious in the past?"

"Once, no twice. A few months ago, right before I was kidnapped, he came by. Then again, not long after I got out of the hospital, I came home and he was at my door. At the time, I thought it seemed suspicious because it looked like he was messing with my lock, but I was also having a mental breakdown right about that time in my life, so I chalked it up to that. He dropped off flowers and let me be. I haven't really heard from him since. I figured he finally got the hint."

Tobin's brow furrows. "I don't like the sound of that. It sounds like he has some stalker qualities. Now, we haven't found anything significant on his record, but that doesn't mean anything."

I lean back in my chair. "What were you doing with Tom yesterday?"

Tobin frowns, visibly jolted by the way I've hijacked the conversation. "I told you."

"I know that, but what else were you doing?"

He leans back, sizing me up. "I'm not sure what you want me to say. I told you already. I made the decision to retrieve your phone. I called him. Let him know through questioning of suspects that he was seen with you, so I asked about your phone. He quickly said that he did have it because you and he had talked in his car. You must have dropped it there. He and I agreed to meet so I could pick it up. While he and I talked, I asked him about that night and if he saw anything suspicious. He didn't. That was that. Afterward, we chatted briefly about old times before he had to run. Your relationship with him or how you two know one another didn't even come up."

"I doubt that."

"Are you saying I'm lying?"

His direct, bold stare has doubt rising inside my center. "I didn't say that. I...I don't know what to think anymore. I'm confused and don't know who to trust. How do I know I can trust you?"

My voice has risen with my growing anxiety and two officers stop to watch our interaction. Tobin gives them a stark glance and they turn away.

He leans forward, lowering his voice. "Listen, Tessa. You've been through the damn wringer lately. The kidnapping. Thinking you're being followed. And now this guy breaking into your apartment. I'm not surprised you're second-

224

guessing yourself about who to trust and not to trust. But have I ever given you any reason not to trust me?"

I swallow down the rising lump in my throat, choking back tears. "No. No, you haven't. Not until now, anyway."

"Exactly, and I don't intend to. And I don't see this as a violation of that trust either. I'm trying my damnedest not to let the fact that I've developed complicated feelings toward you compromise my professional obligations toward you. I have a job to do, and keeping you safe is one of them. I can't let anything get in the way of that."

Feelings toward me? I don't know why, but hearing those words makes me want to cry even more. Why is everything so damn complicated? I shake my head and wave off the comment. "I'm sorry, you're right. It's just been a weird night. We can get back to your questions."

He shakes his head too, as if trying to remember where he was before I derailed the conversation.

Another thought enters my mind. One that I'd never entertained before. "Do you think Gerald had anything to do with my kidnapping? I mean, it's hard to imagine, but he was there that night at the club, and now we find him breaking and entering into my apartment while I'm here, for crying out loud." The intrusive part of the whole incident still has me on edge.

Tobin gives me an apprehensive look, while toying with the pencil in his hand. "We can't jump to those kinds of conclusions. Yet. Although, I've wondered from the beginning and didn't want to say anything that might influence you in any way or add to your anxiety. But given the variety of coincidences and circumstances, he is certainly starting to fit into the category of a likely suspect in the kidnapping. For now, he's for sure going down for breaking and entering. They're searching his home now. I have a feeling it won't be long until we link him to your case. Maybe we finally have our guy."

I take another sip of tea. The idea of closing the case once and for all should offer me a sense of closure, of peace. So why don't I feel it?

CHAPTER TWENTY-THREE

My clothes are soaked through to the skin. Chills course through my body in violent waves. It's more than uncomfortable. It's downright miserable and I desperately want to be home and in the comfort of my bed, sinking into the soft mattress.

Instead, I lurk in the shadows across the street from the building where my support group meets every week. Grace has come to the meetings black and blue almost every week over the past month, her mood dour and dark as opposed to loud and crass. Then last week she didn't show at all. I know her husband's abuse is escalating. It always does. I can't watch in silence anymore so I wait outside the building and pray that she made it tonight. Shivering. Cold. Determined.

Last night's revelations still haunt me. Tom and Tobin talking. Gerald breaking into my home, possibly linked to my kidnapping. My phone sitting in Tom's home. Tobin retrieving it behind my back.

Before he'd done that, I'd already decided to retrieve the phone. Even now that I have it back, I'm still compelled to take a look around Tom's home. I'm not even sure why. Because he lied? Because he kept it from me? I'm not sure but I need to fulfill this compulsion, if even just to get back at him in some weird way. Maybe I'll show up out of the blue, like last time, and catch him off guard. Maybe I'll break in while he's gone. Maybe I'll call ahead and just tell him I've tracked it down to his house and demand it back. The incident with Gerald breaking into my apartment incited a restless agitation that I can't seem to squelch. Even though I know he's sitting in jail with charges against him, and likely more to come in regard to my case, I just can't settle down. I feel off.

I'm jerked back to the present as everyone filters out of the building and disperses quickly to their cars in search of reprieve from the rain, I hold my breath and watch for her familiar form. When she finally walks out, she is moving slower than usual and she holds her left side. I wonder if she has a broken rib or two. Instead of heading toward a car, she turns and makes her way down the sidewalk. She's mentioned before that she lives close by, so I wait until she's a safe distance then step out of the shadows and follow her.

I also happen to know that her husband has bowling league these same nights. He typically waits for her to return home before he leaves so he knows where she is. He also thinks she's at an AA meeting, not a battered-women support group. It pays to be the quiet one who always listens and takes mental notes. Three blocks down, she slowly ascends a few concrete stairs in front of an old apartment building that looks like it's had its share of bad days. I can almost feel her pain as she carefully maneuvers her way up one foot then the other, one stair at a time.

I settle under the eaves of another building kitty-corner across the street. With my arms wrapped tight around my chest, I watch for him to emerge. It feels like forever, and I begin to wonder if I've made a mistake or heard her wrong. Maybe he's not going anywhere this evening. The muscles in my lower back spasm from the cold, wet weather. If I don't stop shivering soon I'm going to have to give up.

Then the front door swings open and a ginormous behemoth of a man steps out of the building. I know it's him by the cocky swagger. I've seen him from afar before when he met her after a meeting. He's been drinking. It's in the way he moves, as if he's having a difficult time coordinating his movements. I wonder how he bowls in such a condition. Then again, he probably does a lot of things in that condition.

He makes his way down the stairs and crosses the street. I avert my gaze and slink against the brick wall, hoping to remain unnoticed.

I watch him climb into an older Ford F150. I move quickly, hunching down and running until I'm close enough to read the license plate. BVZ 796. Color, dark blue. A dent in the back fender and the left tail light is out. Now I know what he drives and where he lives. That's all I needed to know. For now. The rest of the plan will come soon enough. I need to be patient.

Fraught with nervous energy, I know I can't go home. I'll never sleep. I need an outlet for this frustration. I decide to move on to the second goal of my night. Tom's house. I'm driven. Maybe part of me just wants to see him again. That thought is shameful so I push it away. I just want answers. I hop up and rush down the road to my car.

***

The entire house sits in complete darkness, except for a single porch light next to the front door. Even the lamp post by the driveway is out. The driveway is empty, but maybe the cars are in the garage. I sneak along the side of the house, looking for the best possible entrance to the home, keeping an eye out for an alarm system. I've never broken into a house before, or anywhere for that matter. I'm both terrified and thrilled.

I peek into the windows of the garage. It's empty. A sigh of relief escapes my lips. I think he's out for the evening. I need to be quick then. After circling the house, I decide to climb the tree on the right side of the home, as it sits close enough that I think I can make it to the second-story roof. There's a window up top that looks open. With more effort and grunting than I thought I'd need, I claw my way up the tree and scale out onto the farthest limb. Fear wells up and threatens to send me back down and running home. I can't do this. It's too far. I've gone too far this time. It seems to be my pattern lately.

I picture Tom's shitty sneer as he forced me to give him a blow job that night in the car. Then Gerald's sheepish smile and perfect timing as I ran away and right into Jake's trap. How had he known where to find me? These men in my life. How they've made such a fool of me.

I shake my head and reel in my wandering thoughts. Bending at the knees, I crouch down and crawl out further onto the branch so I can hang down from it and swing my body the extra two feet to the roof. It seems so much farther now that I'm up here and I'm not even sure I will make it. Carefully, I lower my body so I'm dangling from the branch, and gently kick my legs out so I can give it a little push. My palms scrape against the bark and burn. Fuck, I need to just jump and get it over with. So I kick back then swing forward, lurching my body toward the roof, praying to God I'll make it. My feet thud onto the roof, then slip. I lunge forward to regain my balance. Falling backward means falling off the house.

On my hands and knees, I hold still and listen to my surroundings for any sign of disturbance. All is silent. I crab-crawl on my hands and feet to the window and hunch close to the house. I was right. The window is completely open. I remember how Tom always had to have a window open when he slept, and I wonder if this is his room. Quietly, I remove the screen and slip inside. The room is quiet and dark, but the moon shines bright enough that I can see the silhouette of a king-sized bed, a television on a dresser along the opposite wall, and three doorways. I find that one leads to a bathroom, another to a closet, and the other to the hall.

Tom's familiar scent wafts up, confirming this is indeed his room. It triggers a slew of memories that make me feel both ashamed and used. It's odd how a smell can do that.

Confident that the house is in fact empty, I move around the room more at ease and begin my random search. For what? I'm still not sure. Maybe I'm simply feeding the alter-ego I've developed lately. Feeding the adrenaline that comes with breaking the rules and facing my fears. After half an hour of senseless rummaging, I grow bored. An underlying anxiety is knocking at the door just behind that boredom. What if I'm caught? I'm frustrated and sweaty, and I'm beginning to fear he'll come home soon.

Distraught but determined, I make my way down the hall, peeking into the remaining rooms upstairs. Another bathroom. One other bedroom that appears stark and lacking personality, like a guest room that has never been occupied. I get the sense that Tom rarely has visitors in his home and I wonder why he's so private. It always hurt my feelings that he refused to invite me over, but then again, I was too meek to ask.

At the end of the hall, I open the last door to what looks like an office. Moonlight spills into this room directly, offering more visibility. A desk sits to the left. Cabinets line one wall. A recliner sits in the corner, facing a television along the opposite wall. This is where he hangs out the most. I feel it. I search through the desk and come up empty. Papers, file folders, a set of keys, and other innocuous items

232

fill the drawers. I turn to see a mid-sized metal cabinet in the corner. About three feet wide, it stands as tall as me. It piques my interest. What secrets does it hold? Circular key holes stare back at me. Curious, I turn back to the desk and rifle through in search of those keys.

The first and second key I try doesn't work, but the third slips right in. It sticks, but after a little jiggle, it finally turns. Disappointment fills my center when I open the doors and see that the contents are a boring let down. It's full of DVDs. From one end to the other. Why would he have them locked up? I step forward and take a better look. They're blank covers with only numbers on the side. Black and plain-looking. Homemade. Private, sexy videos, I wonder. Then I remember the time he begged me to let him record us when we made love. He'd rented a room in our favorite hotel and I'd agreed after he promised he'd never let anyone see it.

Mortified, I pulled out a few of the discs and wonder which one is mine. With my heart in my throat, I turn toward the television and slip one of the DVDs into the player. I take two steps back, waiting for the screen to come alive, while my ears strain for any outside noise that might alert me.

A room flashes into view. A single bed sits in the middle. A girl lies on the bed, still, as if sleeping. My soul turns to ice. I know this scene. It's a different bed, a different room, a different girl, but it's the same scene. My hands shake and my knees give out so that I fall forward, but my eyes never leave the screen. I hit fast forward then hit play randomly and watch as men I don't recognize beat a frail, young woman. She screams and begs. I hit stop and scramble across the floor to vomit into a small waste basket by the desk, vile sour phlegm clogs my airway so that I choke and chortle. When I'm done I sit back on my haunches then fall backward. I'm shaking so hard I can't stand. I'll never get out of here.

I wipe sour bile from my lips and turn toward the other DVDs. Are all of them like this one?

I know they are. White heat sears up through the center of my core as revelation after revelation reverberate throughout my mind and set my core on fire. It wasn't Gerald. It never was. Tom was at the club that night. He lured me out to his car. He knew I'd run off. Right into his trap. Fucking Tom!

I have to get the hell out of here. I make sure to put everything back where I found it, lock the cabinets, put the keys away. I pull the small trash bag of puke out of the waste basket and tie it up, taking it with me down the hall, through Tom's bedroom and out the window. I can't get down the way I came up, so I slide on my belly to the edge of the roof and dangle as far down as I can before letting go. I fall hard, my ankles jarring forcefully as I hit the ground and stumble backward to my bottom. Pain shoots up my legs but I ignore it and scramble to my feet, running as fast as my legs will carry me from this place.

***

Haven't slept all night. After retreating to my

234

apartment, I tried. Desperately, I tried to push away what I discovered for just a little bit so I could sleep. I might have dozed here and there, but mostly, I stared at the ceiling and processed the horror of it all. To say the least, I'm shaken up from what I found at Tom's and I need to think over what to do about it. I roll out of bed and pace the house for hours, biting on my nails. I'm sick to myself. Just sick. But I'm paralyzed about what to do about my findings. Do I go to the police? Call Tobin? What if I'm wrong? Just because he has tapes like those doesn't mean he's to blame. Maybe he's just a sick motherfucker. I shake my head. No, I know he's to blame, somehow. I just do. It's no coincidence.

I'm also not entirely sure about how much I can trust Tobin these days. I hate to admit that to myself. I have feelings for him. But since the day I saw him with Tom, I'm just not sure who or what to believe anymore. What if he had something to do with the whole thing from the beginning? The only person I'm sure of these days is myself. And even that's a little iffy. Frazzled and sketched out, I decide to take a walk to clear my mind. When I step outside, I'm almost shocked that it's so late in the afternoon. I lost most of the day stressing about what I found. No wonder my mind is fried. I wander the streets, oblivious to everything around me as memories of my kidnapping come forth fresh into my mind. It feels like a whole new violation to think that Tom was at the core of it all along. It's so confusing. Had he been vetting me to be his victim the entire time we were dating?

Well over an hour later, I'm freezing and wet. I've accomplished nothing. I want to go home. On the way, I pass a small internet café. The red **'OPEN'** sign blinks at me and the warm yellow glow of the lights inside beckon me in. There's nothing at the apartment. I haven't shopped in weeks. It looks so warm and the sound of a hot cup of coffee is impossible to resist. I make note of my appearance: workout clothes, North Face fleece jacket, baseball cap. I look like any other Pacific Northwesterner, out and about in the dreary weather. Wet and looking for shelter.

I slip inside and make a beeline for the counter. I'll be in and out.

The small café is even warmer than I anticipated, with a strong smell of cinnamon wafting over the humid air. Only three people sit inside, all of them distracted by laptops or cell phones, lost in the technological abyss of our world. Two look like students, probably studying for finals. The other is an older gentleman, hunched over his phone while sipping on something hot. The warm air embraces me and a wave of sleepiness washes over, as well. My lids grow heavy. I should go home and sleep.

A television hovers in the top right corner behind the counter, mounted high on the wall. A weatherman describes the next week of rain using as many different nouns as possible to seem interesting. Rain showers, drizzle, thunderstorms, mist. It's all fucking rain. Who cares?

A petite redhead steps to the counter. "Good evening. What can I get for you?"

I drag my eyes off the screen and try to focus. "A

236

sixteen-ounce hot cocoa, please."

"Will that be all?"

"Yes, thank you."

"Another Western Washington woman goes missing..."

My head jerks up to focus on the television as another reporter stands outside of what looks like a college campus. The background is dark, so I assume it was filmed the night before.

"Yes, Melinda. I'm standing in front of Bellevue Community College this evening talking with student Sarah Matheson, who has reported witnessing a possible kidnapping earlier this evening."

More awake than moments before, I hold my breath, staring up at the screen, a deep ache settling in my chest as they cut to a college student. Her eyes are wide set as she stares directly into the camera, a look of fright supporting the fear she feels. "So, yeah, I'm taking night classes because I work during the day. I don't get out until eight fifty, so by then the parking lot is pretty quiet. When I reached my car, I heard what sounded like a shout, like someone yelling for help, but it was muffled. I turned and at first didn't see anything, but then I noticed there was a car at the far end of the lot, under a maple tree. It blocked the streetlight, so it was pretty dark, but I could see that there were two people and it appeared they were struggling. The larger of the two shoved the smaller one into the passenger door, then ran to the other side and hopped in. I'm pretty sure the smaller one was a woman, and she sounded female when she yelled."

"So you actually heard the woman cry for help? Do you think it was a couple fighting? Did you hear what they were saying or get the make of the car?"

"I'm not sure if it was a couple arguing, but it looked as if the woman was really fighting him. It was scary. And it was pretty dark, and I'm not good with cars, but I told the police that it was either black or navy blue, and it was a two-door, like maybe a Prius, except maybe not that fancy."

They cut back to the news reporter. "Police are investigating Sarah's account to verify whether or not it was indeed a kidnapping. Due to the recent kidnappings locally, they are taking accounts such as these very seriously. They are looking to see if there have been any reports of a missing woman, though it's only been a few hours, so it's unlikely anyone would have made any such reports at this time."

I turn away from the television, the sounds around me blurring together. Am I dreaming? Terin takes night classes at Bellevue Community College. She drives a black two-door Subaru. It's just a coincidence. It's not her. But I haven't heard from her since the day before yesterday, either...I need my damn phone, but I left it behind, again. I'm not used to carrying it these days. I turn to the customer sitting three stools down from me. "Excuse me, sir?"

The older gentleman glances up from his phone and offers a raised brow my direction. "Yes?"

"I'm sorry to bother you, but would you allow me to borrow your cell phone for just a moment? It's a bit of an emergency."

He looks at the phone in his hand, clearly reluctant to hand it over. Then shrugs and leans over, his hand outstretched. "I guess, but don't mess with my *Bejeweled* game."

I stand and grasp the phone. "Of course. I won't touch your game. It'll just take me one minute."

Time slows down and barely moves as I hold the phone to my ear and wait an eternity while the empty rings echo on the other side. Hope rises when Terin's spastic voice comes over the line, then quickly plummets as I realize it's just her recorded greeting. I hang up and redial. Three times. The man stares at me with growing impatience. I let the last recording play out and wait for the beep.

"Hey, Ter, just me. Damn it, I wish I had my phone. I'll try your work number." Ignoring the way the man stirs in his chair and clears his throat, I dial Terin's work number. It's almost two in the afternoon. She'd better be there. As it rings, I turn away so I don't have to watch the way the man glares at me.

"Northwest Property Management Group. This is Barbara, how may I help you?"

"Hi, Barbara. This is Tessa. I'm trying to reach Terin. Do you think you could put her on the line for me?"

"Well, I would, but she didn't come in today. Kind of odd too, because she hasn't called in and she had a meeting this afternoon that she missed. Not like her to do that. I'm assuming she'll be in tomorrow, though. Can I put you through to her voicemail so you can leave a message?"

The world tilts and I feel like I might pass out.

"She didn't come in?" I ask in a low whisper, more to myself than to Barbara. "No, no voicemail. Thanks, bye." Before she can answer, I hit the end call button and hand it over. "Thanks."

I can't take it. I turn and bolt out of the café.

I run down the street. It's a long walk to my apartment, but I can make it in just over ten minutes if I run. I need my car. My wet clothes cling to my skin, strangling me. Terin's beguiling face chases after me. I know she's out there. Terrified. Somehow, I think she's the next one. I killed Vance and Jake. Still, the man who hired them remains, and he could have hired a couple of other Jakes and Vances. Could it really have been Tom? After tonight, I know it had to have been. Whoever it was, he's out there. Wanting his next film. Thirsty for it.

Maybe I'm crazy, but I don't think so. She's his next victim. Even if she's not, we all know it won't end well. I cringe, thinking of her next few hours or days. It is one of violence and terror. I want to pull my hair out. I want to scream. I can't stand the idea that I know her fate.

CHAPTER TWENTY-FOUR

Pacing, pacing, pacing. I bite my nails to the quick and continue to pace my living room. My hands shake. It's almost three in the afternoon and after being up most of the night and all damn day, I need sleep, but I can't even stand to lie down for more than a minute or two. After checking Terin's apartment and all her common hangouts, she remains nowhere to be found. I should call Tobin. I should report her as the missing woman. But I'm afraid his questioning will slow me down. I'm afraid he won't believe anything I'd tell him about Tom. And even if I did trust Tobin, how can I turn over the search to a slow, bureaucratic process, knowing that Terin is out there somewhere, suffering?

I need to find a way to fix it. *Think*. I run a hand through my hair and plop down in the middle of the living room floor, muttering to myself. *Think, it's okay, it's gonna be okay, think*. Thoughts jumble together, weaving in and out, almost making sense at times, and then spreading out into thin, incoherent fragments. Who am I kidding? This is hopeless. No one can save her.

But I have to. I have to find her.

On my belly, I drag the small box out from under my bed, hitting my head on the frame as I slither backward. Barely fazed, I sit back on my haunches and open the box. Before, this godforsaken SD card represented nothing but horror to me. Now…I pray that it has answers. I wish I had thought to grab some or all of the DVDs from Tom's house. I guess I'm still on a learning curve as a criminal.

In my living room, I sit on the couch and watch every painful moment, reliving it all over again. I tremble. The girl on the screen is unrecognizable to me. I no longer understand her. She cries. She sleeps. She doesn't fight back, not at first anyway. And now, when I watch her, all I see is Terin in her same position. Somewhere out there. Behind all of it is Tom. Other than the videos I found in his home, I don't have proof that he is linked to my kidnapping, but I know it beyond a doubt. Disgust weeps from my bones. He will pay, I'll make sure of that. But right now, I have to find her.

I try to ignore the woman on the screen and focus on listening to all conversation, hoping Jake or Vance will say something that offers a clue.

The scene where they hose me down plays out. I cringe, remembering the frigid water, the humiliation. As I walk back into the cabin, it looks even smaller than I remember. Hatred seethes through every pore of my body. I'll burn that damn cabin down someday. Burn it to the ground.

Vance's handheld camera work is amateur at best, and I feel motion-sick just from watching the jerky footage. He follows the girl through the cabin and into the claustrophobic bedroom where a single bed sits. Jake leads the way. The girl shivers and cries, mumbling incoherent sentences, her shoulders hunched in defeat as she scuffles to the bed and lies down in the fetal position. Broken. I want to slap her.

Jake glances down at his clothing. "Shit, I'm all wet." His brow furrows but his tone remains flat. "Look what you did. Now I have to change." Without another word, he stomps out of the room. It's déjà vu as the entire scene plays out before me.

The room bounces and spins as Vance crosses the room and places the camera back on the tripod in the corner. The image stabilizes like a sailor finally setting foot on land.

The girl lies on the bed, comatose, as Vance marches out of the room and returns minutes later with a wool blanket on hand. He crouches beside her and covers her with it.

Jake's raspy voice bellows out from the other room. "Why the fuck did we have to use this damn place? There's no bathroom and no running water inside the cabin. What the hell?"

Vance stands and walks to the doorway. "Because the boss said we had to stay away from the other place. He didn't say why, but I'm guessing he doesn't want the last two girls linked in any way. I don't know why he's worried about it, though. He owns both cabins. They're his private property and they're under another name. No one's going to find either place. He's just paranoid. If you ask me, the fucker is crazy. Why else would he hire anyone to do this shit?"

Jake responds, but he's no longer yelling, and I can't make out what he's saying. Vance leaves the room. The girl sleeps.

I turn it off. I have what I need. Tom has another cabin and I need to find out where it is. I chew on my lower lip and weigh out my options. Should I call Tobin and tell him what I know? Maybe he could help me find the cabin. I shake my head. I can't imagine the police handling this the right way. Not my way, anyway.

I have to get back inside Tom's house. I'll find the location of the other cabin there. I'm not sure I can bear it knowing that Terin is out there. Time is our enemy. I can't wait. I'll have to take a chance and go now. God willing, he'll be gone.

***

My leg muscles cramp and quiver, threatening to give out as I crouch low in a closet in one of the upstairs spare bedrooms. Sweat drips down my spine and into the crevice of my ass. The air around me feels thick, but I know it's just my own fear. I hesitate to take a deep breath for fear he'll hear me.

I'd been searching his bedroom and the study where I found the videos for the better part of the last hour, and came up empty-handed and frustrated. On my way down the hall with a plan of heading downstairs, I stopped in mid-step when I heard the front door open and a single pair of footsteps enter the home. How had I not heard the car pull up in the driveway?

Now, I hold my breath and pray for guidance as I search my brain for a plan. The irrational side of me wants to bust out of this damn closet and kill that motherfucker with my bare hands. Immediate and exacting revenge. I want it so bad I can taste it. But then I'd never find out where Terin is. He'd never tell me. She'd die before anyone could find her. I can't let that happen.

My legs spasm harder, so I carefully stand and allow the blood to flow back into them. I keep close to the wall. Even though the sliding door of the closet is pulled shut, I still imagine that he can somehow see me.

It feels like a lifetime passes as I hover in my hiding place and listen to the sounds of his footfalls ascending the stairs, retreating to his bedroom, turning on the shower, opening dressers. At nearly four in the afternoon, I'm surprised he's already home. Maybe his schedule alters when he knows one of his victims is out there. Does it give him pleasure? Does he anticipate his prize? How did I ever care for this monster?

Even after the sounds of his movements dissipate and the house settles, I remain stoic in my refuge. My mind runs wild with ideas both desperate and insane. What will benefit Terin?

When I hear his bedroom door close, I assume he's hopping into the shower. Maybe preparing to go out to dinner? I creep out of my hiding place, every movement painfully slow in my effort not to

245

make a single sound. I cringe with every infinitesimal creak of the wood floors beneath my feet. As I approach the top of the stairs, a wave of dizziness overtakes me and I grasp the railing. I take in two, slow deep breaths, and realize I've been holding my breath too long. When I recover, I start the steady descent down the stairs, begging the universe for mercy.

When I reach the bottom, I pause, disoriented. I've never been here before. I peek around one wall and see an open-concept living room and a kitchen with vaulted ceilings. I know the garage is on that side of the home as well.

Peering around the other direction, I see there is another living space. I take a step down and feel plush carpet beneath my sneakers. A massive television and stereo system line one wall. Cush leather recliners sit opposite. This is his entertainment area. A short hallway leads out of the room. I tiptoe across and down the hall. A guest bathroom sits to the right. At the end is another doorway. I imagine another bedroom. It takes every muscle in my body to turn that doorknob as slowly and quietly as possible. I feel like I might pass out before I'm done with this escapade of mine.

As the door opens, I'm surprised to see an oddly tiny and cramped space, not quite large enough to quantify as a bedroom but not quite small enough to be a closet. I close the door behind me, then turn and address the contents of the room. A few boxes are stacked in the left corner. A huge, burdensome armoire stands with fortitude against the wall. Likely an old heirloom passed down over generations. Beautifully crafted seventeenth-century-style swords and knives of various size decorate one wall. The other wall is full of a vast display of framed paintings. There's very little wall left visible. It's overdone and gaudy. Most disturbing are the images.

All of them convey the same terrifying images of blood lust, sacrifice, and gratuitous violence. I feel the blood from my upper body drop down to my toes as another wave of vertigo overpowers me. I lower myself to the floor and put my head between my knees. What is wrong with this man? How does someone become such a demonic savage?

When I'm able to stand again, I make my way to another large cabinet that stands against the third wall. It's covered in intricate carvings, and when I step closer to inspect it further, I'm disturbed by more violence etched into the wood. Gothic pictures of what looks like ancient blood sacrifices and rituals decorate what would otherwise be a lovely piece of furniture. This entire room gives me the creeps. And yet another window into Tom's multi-spectrum persona.

A creak of the floor above me causes the hair on the back of my neck to stand up. I freeze and wait for any further sounds. The silence is deafening. I resume my inspection of the room and open the doors of the carved cabinet. The doors are heavy and swing open. I'm surprised to see more artifacts that look like ancient relics of the Middle Ages. Desperate to hurry and be on my way, I close the doors and turn toward the armoire. I'm surprised to see that there are filing cabinets built inside of it. So

247

odd.

I pull one drawer out at a time and see that there are numerous types of documents inside. One is labeled **PASSPORT AND IDENTIFICATION**. Another is labeled **INSURANCE**. A third is labeled **MOTHER'S ESTATE AND WILL**. These are Tom's personal documents. My heart skips a beat as hope rises. I open the next set of files and see two more labels. One says **DEBTS**. The other says **ASSETS**.

With shaky hands I thumb through the **ASSETS** file and hit gold. Bank statements, mortgage papers, financial transactions, tax history. Growing anticipation of what I'm about to find brings on another bout of dizziness and I take deep breath. Finally, I find multiple pieces of paper with **WELLS FARGO FINANCIAL** at the top of each. The top section is paper-clipped together and has this home address listed with Tom Hastings, the third as the owner. The second group of paper-clipped papers is the cabin on Goat Mountain. That's where Jake and Vance had taken me. The third is another property listed without a specific address. Both are listed under Benjamin Ashford.

My heart thuds in my chest. Where have I heard that name before?

Tobin mentioned it the day he came by my apartment. He'd said they found the name of who owned the cabin. An alias. Benjamin Ashford. Goddammit! Hot tears well up. I can't stand to think of Terin out there while I'm rummaging around in here putting the puzzle pieces together.

Hold on, Terin. Hold on. I'm coming.

Panic rises as I search the documents for an

248

address to the second property and find the only reference of location as Williput Creek. The last page is a printout from Google Maps. I sigh with relief and wipe my tears away.

I have what I need. Now I need to get the hell out of here. Before it's too late.

CHAPTER TWENTY-FIVE

Breathe in. Breathe out. My knuckles are white and achy from gripping the steering wheel so tight. Not from fear, but from rage. Fury and a hunger for revenge consume me. In my mind's eye I see everything Terin must be going through. I feel her terror in a way that most other humans will never experience.

I hold my cell phone to my ear and count each ring, praying he'll pick up. Praying I'm making the right decision by trusting him now. This is his moment to prove himself. His voice is thick with sleep when he finally does. "Hello?"

"Tobin? Were you sleeping?"

"Yeah, I have a night shift tonight, so I was napping."

"Thank God you picked up. I need your help."

"Tessa? Are you okay?"

I can picture him sitting up in bed, a worried expression on his handsome face. It hits me hard that he really does care for me. I tuck that away.

"I'm fine but I need your help."

"My help? Of course. Tell me what's going on."

"It's not Gerald." I go into the whole story, breaking down the chain of events that led me to Tom's house and what I've discovered. I talk so fast I can barely catch my breath. Tobin sits quietly on the other end of the line, and I wonder if he's still there, but I can't stop. Every word waits anxiously on the tip of my tongue, desperate for release.

"We have to help her, Tobin. We have to get to her before it's too late."

"Tom. Fuck. Okay, yeah, of course we do. And you said you have a map?"

"Yes, I'm on my way there now. Before it gets dark." I wait for him to get pen and paper, then rattle off the directions into the phone. "I need you and your men to meet me out there."

"What? No. Wait. You're not going out there, Tessa. Let us handle this."

"It might be too late by then. I'm already on my way. I'm not standing on the sidelines while those sick bastards do God only knows what to my best friend. I just can't."

Tobin's voice lowers, his tone conveying a suppressed emotion. Fear? Anger? Both? "Listen, Tess, I know that this hits close to home for you, and it's bringing up stuff that I can't even begin to imagine. But that's exactly why you can't go out there. You're not rational. You'll put you and your friend in even more danger. Just turn around and go home and let me do my job."

"I'm sorry. I can't."

I pull the phone away and look at the display screen. Before my thumb hits the button, I hear Tobin's faraway plea. "Goddammit! Tessa, don't—" *Click.*

The computerized voice of a female on my GPS system calls out the next set of directions. *"Up ahead, take the next left onto Williput Creek Road."*

Anticipation swells within me. I glance toward the passenger seat to see my dad's old hunting rifle propped up against the window. It's been years since I handled it, but I still remember everything he taught me.

My focus returns to the road ahead. I lean forward, close to the steering wheel, and peek up at the sky. A grayish-pink hue decorates the horizon as dusk approaches. The drive up the mountain took a lot longer than anticipated. The paved highway gave way to gravel mountain roads a ways back and now I feel the isolation of my surroundings. No wonder there is no address for the cabin. Just a spot on the map.

As directed, I look for the next left. The GPS shows that I'm practically upon it but I don't see the road until I'm only about fifty feet from it. It sits obscure, just a worn dirt road with forest and thick underbrush on both sides. An old sign reads 'WILLIPUT CREEK ROAD.' I hit the brakes and swerve onto the single-lane path marked out only by parallel tire grooves. The farther down the road I get, the taller the grass is on the sides. Down the middle, it's overgrown. The car bumps and bounces over the rough terrain and I wish I had a four-wheel drive.

I come to a fork in the road. One continues on to the left and appears similar to the road I've been on, with the same amount of wear and tear. The one that veers off to the right looks hardly used, and overgrown to the point I can barely make out the tire paths. Instinct tells me it's the more nebulous of the two. A well-hidden and camouflaged hiding place.

I turn the wheel and make my way down the path. Though it's overgrown, I can tell the road has been used recently by the way the tops of the grass shoots bend in the direction I'm going. Nervous tension grips my belly, and for the first time I'm overwhelmed with doubt. What am I doing? Can I do this? What if I fail? Images of a frightened woman tied to a bed, riddled with fear, and stripped of her dignity flash over and blanket the doubt. It doesn't matter whether my plan works or not. What matters is that I try. I'll die trying if needed.

Up ahead the road looks like it opens to a field. I pull off the trail and into the tall grass. I don't want them to hear me coming, so I'll walk the rest of the way. I can only assume there are two of them, as there were with me, but I just don't know. Darkness is consuming the last bit of daylight quicker than I'm comfortable with, adding a sense of urgency. I reach across the seat, my fingers wrapping around cold steel, before I slide out of the vehicle. I feel flushed, fevered. Heat rises within me, boiling my blood with a visceral need to set things right.

As I approach the clearing, a wood building comes into view off to the right. The depravity of it sends a shiver up my spine. It's not even a house.

It's merely a rundown shelter of sorts. The kind of thing thrown together in haste. Four walls surrounded by two-foot-high grass shoots and dirt. It's quiet. Too quiet. And there's no car in sight. Terin went missing over twenty-four hours ago. A sinking feeling overwhelms me. Am I too late?

Darting forward, I hunch low, bending my knees while cutting through the grass to reach the shelter. At the door, I hesitate. I want to look inside before I barrel in. I want to know what I'm up against. I round the corner. There are no windows. I circle quietly, making my way around the building. A broken board about hip height pokes out from the back corner. I sidle up to the wood planks and kneel down, pressing my face against the dusty wood. It takes a moment for my eyes to adjust.

At first, I see only a stark room with dirt floors. Streams of light filter down through breaks in the ceiling, revealing thick dust floating in the air. A table sits to the right of the door with various items spewed over it, but I can't make out the details of what they are. The center of the room is bare. My heart skips a beat when I finally see a blinking red light on the far side of the room. My mouth goes dry, and I have a hard time swallowing. Everything that camera represents threatens to break me all over again. It points toward the corner I'm perched at. Shifting my weight, I try to peer in at an angle to see the area it focuses on.

At first I see nothing. I press my face harder against the wood and squint to get a better look. There. Something in the corner, on the floor. Two bare feet. I can see what looks like a woman's dainty legs but I can't see past her upper thighs. Bare thighs. They lie limp.

Please don't be dead.

I pull away, my breath shallow and quick, mulling over my options. Her captors are gone. I can't imagine them leaving for long at all if she's alive.

Panic engulfs me.

Fuck, I'm too late.

I stand and waver as the blood rushes to my head from crouching so long. Before I fully recover, I start toward the front of the building, my gun clenched tight by my side. The front door lacks a handle, so I push it open. It squeaks and sunlight spills over my shoulder into the dim room. The lifeless body lays in a heap in the corner. I rush to her side and bend down and pull the hair away from her face. It sticks to her cheek, crusty with her own blood and filth. Her face is black and blue and swollen from her beatings. My heart breaks. Rage seethes through the sadness as tears spill down my cheeks.

My friend. My beautiful friend.

I glance over her body as she lies on her side, naked and broken. Under the dirt and bruises her skin is creamy porcelain and soft. I fall onto my ass and stare up at the ceiling, sobbing out loud to the universe. "Why, why, why?"

"Fuck you!" I don't know who I'm yelling at. Is it these atrocious men? Is it God? Am I yelling at myself? "Fuck you!" I kick my feet out and continue to scream and cry out in agony.

My foot makes contact with Terin's lifeless leg

and she moans.

I draw my foot back and scramble to my hands and knees. Bending low, I place my face close to hers and listen for breath. I can't hear anything or feel warmth from her lips. I touch my fingers to her arm. Her skin is cool but not cold. Gently, I find the spot on her inner wrist and feel for a pulse. It takes a second, but my heart races when I feel a thready, weak beat against my fingers.

She's still alive. Thank God. They've left her for dead.

My hands shake as I gently roll her to her back. "Can you hear me? I'm here. Don't be afraid. You're going to be okay."

Her eyelashes flutter but she doesn't open her eyes. I strip out of my thin jacket and lay it over her body, rubbing my hands vigorously over her arms and legs to stimulate her. She moans again, and this time her eyes flitter open, swimming around as she struggles to focus on her surroundings. The pupils dilate. She appears drugged.

"Tessa?"

"You're all right. Just hang in there. Help is on the way."

She mumbles incoherently.

I lean closer. "What? Say it again."

Her head lolls listlessly to the side but she uses her strength and glances up at me with crossed eyes. "Coming…back."

At barely a whisper, I can still make it out. I turn and take in my surroundings. "They're coming back? Are you sure?" I hunch over and look her in the face. "How many are there?"

Her eyes roll back in the sockets and it looks as if she's passed out. Then the eyes flutter again but don't open. She whispers, "One. Just one."

Again, I sit back and take in my surroundings. With daylight nearly gone, visibility is waning. I need to get her out of here. She needs a doctor. I'm guessing she may be bleeding internally and suffering from God only knows what other injuries. And hypothermia is settling in too.

Before I decide what my next step will be, the door of the shack flies open and a male figure bursts through the door.

"What the hell?"

I reach for my gun and leap to my feet as he hurls himself across the room. Before I'm fully upright, his hefty weight slams into my body and knocks me to the floor. My head hits the floor with a sick thud and the room spins as I try to remain conscious. Terin groans. Blind, I kick and struggle to push the man away from me, but his arms are locked around my waist and I'm unable to find leverage against his weight. When he lets go and sits up, he reaches for my neck. As his hands wrap around their target, I buck up with my hips as hard as I can, like Tobin taught me. As his body lurches forward with the momentum, he loses his grip and his balance. I seize the opportunity to roll out from under him. But as I roll away, he grabs my waist again. Now I'm at an angle to him and can reach around, wrapping my bicep around his neck. He fights. I twist and wriggle my body, fighting him with every ounce of my strength, every bit of my will, every drop of my unleashed fury. Finally, I

257

find myself clinging to his side, one arm cinched tight against his throat as he writhes to regain control.

Flashes of my last lesson with Tobin spring forward. *Hold on and don't let go*, Tobin whispers in my ear.

He kicks and punches in an effort to break away. Blows hit my ribs and stomach, and I think I may pass out, but I can't let go. I bring my other arm around and use it to cinch the other arm tighter around his airway. He spits and sputters but continues to fight. I close my eyes and use all of my strength.

I know if I can just outlast him, I will win.

The blows to my core finally lessen in strength. Guttural, desperate sounds strain from his lips. Even when his body slackens and his grip falls away, I keep my arms tight around his neck. I'm not sure how long I hold his body against my own, but when I open my eyes, it feels like time has stopped. Silence engulfs the shack. The only sound I hear is the relentless pounding of my heart in my ears. I release his form and let him fall to the side on the dirt floor.

I glance toward Terin. She moans quietly in the corner. Sirens scream out in the distance. Tobin is on his way. I crawl over the man's body and pick up my gun. I look to the camera across the room. I stand and face it, imagining Tom on the other side, though I know he's not there. I march toward it, stopping just inches before it so that he sees my face clearly.

I stare into the lens, angry and vengeful, and

deliver my message.

CHAPTER TWENTY-SIX

A knocking on the door jolts Tom out of a blissful dream state. He rolls over and looks at the clock. Five in the morning. He grumbles and pulls the covers over his head, hoping he imagined the knocking and wishing the blissful dream to return.

Pound, pound, pound.

"Fuck!" Tom tosses the covers to the side and crawls out of bed, eager to put a stop to the pounding at his door. "Who the fuck is knocking at my door at this time of morning?" he grumbles, tying his robe as he descends the stairs with eyes still half shut.

He peeks through the peephole on the front door. Faint daylight reveals an empty doorstep. Swearing under his breath, he unlocks the door and peeks out. No one is there. The neighborhood is quiet. His neighbors are sleeping. As he closes the door, he glances down and sees an object on the stoop.

He pauses and bends down to pick it up. It's an

SD card for a camera. Just like the one he's used to receiving, but not like this. Not delivered in this manner. His heart skips a beat with anticipation. He snatches the card and takes another look over the neighborhood to makes sure no one is watching before he slams the door closed.

He rushes up the stairs to his study, where he always watches his private videos. He wonders what is going on while he locks the office door and prepares to watch the contents of the card. Knowing his current victim was out there, he'd been expecting a card soon, but not quite yet.

In his robe, he sits in the leather recliner and waits on the edge of his seat for the screen to come alive. At first, he's confused. A girl lies in a heap in the dark corner of the room. The girl he's targeted so perfectly this time. As payback for Tessa's escape.

He wonders why the video has skipped ahead. He grasps the remote and tries to rewind, but it appears he's at the beginning of the footage. Where's the rest of it? The beginning? Anger wells up. This guy fucked it all up. He's erased all of the video. "Shit, stupid asshole."

He hits play and waits to see what is left of the video. When another woman cuts across the room and approaches the body of the woman, he holds his breath. "What in the hell is this?" he utters quietly and scoots to the edge of his seat.

He leans forward, narrowing his gaze, taking in what he's witnessing.

"Oh, fuck." He recognizes the woman. "Tessa?"

He shifts uncomfortably in his seat, inching

261

forward so that he's barely in the chair. His lips part in astonishment as he watches Tessa cry and scream, distraught over her friend's body. Then she is attacked by the man he hired to do the job. Fascination and horror intertwine as the scene unfolds. A nightmare coming to life before his very eyes. How did she get in there? Will he watch her die finally? Is this the unexpected surprise? If so, he will have to pay more for this grisly twist.

The blood drains from his face as he watches their struggle and Tessa gradually overcomes her attacker. Her face is red, her expression haunting, as she closes her eyes and strangles to death the man he hired. In his cabin.

When she drops his body to the floor, Tom gasps and slides off the chair to his knees. "No, no, no."

Tessa crawls to her gun, picks it up, and faces the camera. She marches forward and leans into the camera. Tom leans in, as if she is face to face in the room with him and he is desperate yet terrified to hear what she has to say.

The sound of sirens wail off in the distance, breaking into the horror of what is unfolding here in his study. He hears it filter in like a bad dream but can only focus on the woman on the screen.

"Tom, look at me."

Tom leans forward as Tessa beckons. Lured by her demand. Her eyes are wild, her short choppy hair in disarray. He barely recognizes her from the feeble, weak woman she once was, to this fierce, frightening woman filled with fury.

He looks her in the eyes and shivers. Impending doom knocks on his door.

"Tom. You sick motherfucker. Your time is up. I could come there and kill you myself, but this is so much better. You're going to rot in a prison and become some angry fucker's bitch. It's going to be long, and painful, and oh so deserved. And I...I will haunt your dreams forever."

He shakes his head in disbelief as the sirens grow louder. He looks around the room, contemplating his escape. The sirens are real and closing in fast. Just down the street.

"Tom."

Unable to resist, he turns and listens again.

She pauses, then slowly, a grin widens her pretty mouth. He trembles.

"We're coming for you." It's a whisper this time, but she might as well have screamed it, because it slams into him like a freight train. The screen goes blank.

Tom turns and darts toward the door, scrambling to unlock it. The sirens scream louder and he knows they're out front. As he rushes to his bedroom, police bust through the front door yelling for him to *stop, lie on the ground face first, hands out to the side.*

Every option imaginable races through his mind: *run, fight, suicide.* His vision clouds and blurs as the unimaginable occurs and men tackle him and wrestle him to the ground. Shame and fear overwhelm his senses. He begs for it to all be a dream. He begs for death.

"It wasn't me. This is a mistake," he pleads, knowing it's to no avail. He's been caught. He always knew he would be.

263

As they haul him to his feet and shove him down the stairs and out the front door, he looks for her. He knows she's there. Watching. He sees his old college friend, Tobin, first. Standing by his police car. Keeping a distance as his fellow officers do their job.

When he finally spots her, she is at the edge of the ruckus, standing on the other side of Tobin's car. Her face is unreadable. Stoic and impassive. Only her eyes tell her story. They stare him down with the fire of revenge and the smugness of a battle won.

She uncrosses her arms and lets them fall to her side.

Displayed over her chest, in the center of the t-shirt she wears under a denim jacket, is the symbol of a phoenix rising from its ashes.

ACKNOWLEDGEMENT

I want to give a big Thank You to my sweetheart, Chayne. You came into my life when I was at my lowest and just learning to tap into my own sense of power as a woman and as a single mother. You have been patient and loving, but most of all, you have shown me that men of true integrity do exist.

My family is blessed to have you in our lives. I love you with all of my heart.

ABOUT THE AUTHOR

Michelle King lives in the Pacific Northwest with her four quirky and beautiful children. She loves coffee, Superman, rollercoasters, and has an addiction to chapstick.

She works at a surgery center as a registered nurse and in her spare time writes novels. As a multi-genre author, she has written in the categories of romance suspense, young adult, women's fiction, and literary fiction. She has won four literary awards. You can visit Michelle's website at:

www.authormichelleking.com

Facebook:
https://www.facebook.com/Michelle-King-Author-544448685599147/

Twitter:
https://twitter.com/Michelle_King_1

Website:
www.authormichelleking.com

www.ingramcontent.com/pod-product-compliance
Lightning Source LLC
Chambersburg PA
CBHW030240200626
46816CB00002BA/453